CW01663355

A

TRUSTED

WIFE

(An Emily Just Psychological Thriller —Book 1)

Ella Swift

Ella Swift

Ella Swift is author of the VIVIAN FOX suspense thriller series, comprising five books (and counting); PEYTON RISK mystery series, comprising five books (and counting); of the new COOPER TRACE mystery series, comprising five books (and counting); and of the EMILY JUST psychological thriller series, comprising five books (and counting).

An avid reader and lifelong fan of the mystery and thriller genres, Ella loves to hear from you, so please feel free to visit ellaswiftauthor.com to learn more and stay in touch.

ISBN: 978-1-0943-9853-2

BOOKS BY ELLA SWIFT

PEYTON RISK MYSTERY SERIES
WHAT'S HIS (Book #1)
WHAT'S LEFT (Book #2)
WHAT'S WISHED (Book #3)
WHAT'S GONE (Book #4)
WHAT'S MINE (Book #5)

COOPER TRACE MYSTERY SERIES
SHATTERED MIND (Book #1)
SHATTERED LIFE (Book #2)
SHATTERED HOPE (Book #3)
SHATTERED DREAM (Book #4)
SHATTERED FATE (Book #5)

VIVIAN FOX MYSTERY SERIES
ALL HE TAKES (Book #1)
ALL HE HIDES (Book #2)
ALL HE COVETS (Book #3)
ALL HE NEEDS (Book #4)
ALL HE DESTROYS (Book #5)

EMILY JUST PSYCHOLOGICAL SUSPENSE SERIES
A TRUSTED WIFE (Book #1)
A TRUSTED STRANGER (Book #2)
A TRUSTED HUSBAND (Book #3)
A TRUSTED FRIEND (Book #4)
A TRUSTED NEIGHBOR (Book #5)

PROLOGUE

I can't believe I'm doing this, I think with a thrill of excitement, gazing out the window as we make our way along the streets of San Jose, the largest of the several cities that make up Silicon Valley.

And to think that just a few days ago I was at home, bemoaning my fate, wondering if the universe was forever determined to keep me confined in my hometown of Townsville, Ohio, a cop-out of a name if there ever was one. Nothing, absolutely nothing, happens in Townsville. It's the sort of place where you can predict the weather based on old Mrs. Henderson's arthritis flare-ups, and where the biggest event of the year is the annual bake sale at the church, complete with Mrs. Sweeney's infamous fruit pies.

But here I am, in the heart of technology and innovation, about to play nursemaid to a tech mogul's wife. It sounds like the setup for some quirky indie film, only this is real life.

My life.

I catch my reflection in the window. A mousy girl with tired eyes looks back at me, swallowed by the enormity of her surroundings. I force a smile onto my face, trying to squeeze some confidence into this new version of me.

I can be whoever I want. To these people I am about to meet, I get to be whoever I say I am—which is to say, this is my chance to start over, to reinvent myself.

And maybe even escape the reach of my father's shadow.

My Uber driver, Hernando, a friendly man who has spent most of the drive from the airport regaling me with tales of his native Guatemala, flashes me a warm, understanding smile through the rear-view mirror.

"Excited, Miss Emily?" he asks. He knows the basics of what I'm planning to do, though not all the details. I've never been the type of person to spend much time around someone without striking up a conversation, even if it's a stranger.

"I practically have chills," I reply, my hand unconsciously rubbing at my arm as if to scrub away the goosebumps.

Hernando chuckles. “You will do fine, Miss Emily. You will do fine.”

Catching his eye, I feel a stirring of unease. It's like he can see right through me, through the cloud of happy thoughts, to the troubled waters brewing below. Other people have always had this ability to look past my defenses, no matter how quickly I construct them. I am like a house with too many windows open to the scrutiny of anyone who cares to look inside.

This line of thinking sours the mood, and all the world around me loses color: The emerald green lawns turn a lifeless gray, the vibrant flowers bordering the driveways lose their luster, the faces of the buildings blend into a uniform dullness. How does this happen so quickly? Today was supposed to be about new beginnings, not old fears.

I cast my thoughts back to my last session with Rich a week ago. When I told him about my plan for saving up money so I could pursue my master’s in psychology, he hesitated for just a moment. There was a slight crease to his eyebrows—I have always been good at catching those little details, one of the advantages of having what my mother likes to call a “sensitive nature”—before his face smoothed out again.

“What?” I asked. “What’s wrong?”

“Nothing,” he said a bit too quickly. “What makes you think something’s wrong?”

“I can do this, Rich,” I said, pleading with him to believe in me. “And we can keep in touch with video calls. It’ll be so good for me, you’ll see. I’ll be right next to the Pacific—the Pacific, Rich!—and I'll be able to start fresh, break the cycle. I can make a difference in someone's life."

I thought Rich would be happy for me, but instead he looked troubled, as if he knew something I didn't.

I’m still playing this memory in my mind when Hernando turns the wheel and we head up a long driveway lined with tall pines that sway gently in the afternoon breeze. I look up through the car window at them, and for a moment I feel small, insignificant. It's like being swallowed whole by the world.

"We're here, Miss Emily," Hernando announces, bringing the car to a stop at the entrance of a sprawling manor that looks more like a fortress than a home. Though the sunlight hits it full force, the house seems to drink in the light rather than reflect it, giving off a brooding and somber aura. I am reminded of old gothic novels where decrepit castles hold secrets concealed in their stone hearts.

Of course this is only the effect of my "rabid" imagination, as my mother used to call it with a touch of exasperation whenever she caught me daydreaming. I have always been prone to such flights of fancy. When you grow up in a place as disappointing as Townsville, Ohio, you'd better have a healthy imagination.

Gothic or not, a thrill of excitement courses through me as I take in the grounds around me. There's an elaborate sculpture garden to the right, the marble statues gleaming white against the emerald-green landscape. To the left, a labyrinthine rose garden stretches out as far as I can see, ruby-red blooms peeking through the manicured hedges. And in the distance, the crystalline blue of the Pacific shines like a jewel under the sun's relentless gaze. It's a sight to mesmerize any Midwestern girl far from home.

Hernando opens the car door, and I step out on shaking legs. This is really happening. I'm really doing this.

Look out, world.

I pay Hernando, wishing I had the money to give him a generous tip. I have always been poor—it's practically a family tradition at this point. My mother worked tirelessly to keep us afloat, doing everything from waitressing at the local diner to picking up trash at the theater. She not only taught me what it means to work hard, but what it means to be resilient, even when life seems as harsh and unforgiving as an Ohio winter.

"Thank you, Hernando," I say, meeting his warm brown eyes. There's a quiet understanding there, and for a moment, I feel less alone.

He opens the driver's door and pauses, looking over at the mansion. He is silent for a few seconds—brooding, much like the house itself.

When he looks at me, his eyes are troubled—the same way Rich's eyes were troubled when I told him about my plans. Like they all know something I don't.

"Are you sure you're alright?" he asks.

During the drive, I was the nervous one and he was the one reassuring me it would all work on. Now that we're here, though, the roles seem to have reversed.

"I'll be fine," I say, forcing a lightness into my voice that I do not feel. My fingers clutch the handle of my carry bag a little too tightly, the knuckles white against the worn leather.

Hernando studies me for another moment before he finally nods, his gaze still filled with worry. "Take care, Miss Emily," he says, a touch of fatherly concern in his voice. He disappears back into the car and I watch as it retreats down the long driveway, getting smaller and smaller, leaving me alone here in this new life I have chosen for myself.

Leaving me wondering why everyone else seems to know something I don't.

CHAPTER ONE

As I follow the walkway to the house, I am struck by the utter silence of the place. There is no gardener trimming the roses, no children playing on the lawn, no happy barking of a family dog. Just the faint rustle of leaves beneath my feet and the echo of my own heartbeat pounding in my ears.

Maybe this silence shouldn't come as a surprise, though. The woman I was hired to assist, Alicia Sterling, hasn't left her home in years, I'm told, and it seems fitting that a woman so afraid of the outside world would covet silence.

After all, what is noise but an intrusion on the senses?

I notice a neighbor out carrying the mail up his seemingly interminable driveway. He is rather gnomish, with a newsboy cap and corduroy slacks, and he clutches at his beard as he walks, running his fingers through it nonstop.

"Hello!" I call in a burst of friendliness, waving my hand like a pennant. He slows long enough to regard me, but he makes no acknowledgment. He simply goes on his way as if I wasn't there at all.

Strange. Oh, well. Perhaps he's someone famous and doesn't like being approached by strangers.

I shake off the strange moment and continue toward the Sterling house.

Turning the corner, I come upon the main entrance, an intimidating set of double doors carved with intricate designs. Overhead, a dark orb watches me—a camera, by the look of it. I shouldn't be surprised—I was told the Sterlings were obsessed with technology, and besides, this is Silicon Valley—but the sight of it still sends a shiver down my spine. It's as if the house itself is sentient, watching and judging my…what? Worthiness to enter?

Before I can gather enough courage to ring the bell, the door swings open, revealing a woman in her fifties with a friendly smile. "You must be Miss Just," she says, offering a hand. "I'm Lena Brooks, the housekeeper. Welcome."

Her hand is warm, unlike my own clammy palms. "Thank you, Ms. Brooks." I smile back at her, hoping she doesn't sense the nervous energy radiating off me.

"Please, call me Lena. I know my age, but that doesn't mean I have to be reminded all the time."

She chuckles, and I find myself laughing along, grateful for the moment of lightness. "Alright, Lena," I say, my voice steadier than I feel.

She guides me into the house, and for a moment I am rendered breathless by its grandeur. Tall vaulted ceilings. A lavish staircase spiraling elegantly to the second floor. Long, opulent draperies cascading from enormous floor-to-ceiling windows. It's overwhelming, but beautiful—in a distant, unreachable way.

But what catches my attention the most is the silence: It's a living entity in here, creeping into every corner and residing there like a permanent resident. I feel like an intruder on the silence, as if my mere presence has violated some sacred pact between the house and its occupants.

Lena must sense my awe because she chuckles softly. "You get used to it," she says, her voice reverberating against the marble walls. "I felt the same way at first when I started here. After a while, you grow used to it. The silence becomes almost…companionable."

Despite her words, I can't help but think that Lena's eyes hold a certain sadness nestled within the laughter.

With a swift turn of her heel, she begins to guide me through the mansion's labyrinthine corridors. The rooms we pass are grand and tastefully decorated, every piece of furniture and art exuding an air of effortless wealth. Yet not one room gives away any hint of personal touch, no family photos or trinkets—nothing to indicate that a family lives here.

Like a silk jacket still hanging on the manikin.

"When was it you started working here?" I ask as we walk. I have already become thoroughly lost—if it were up to me to find my way out, I might wander for hours before reaching the front door again.

Lena, her posture alert (almost military, one might say), answers immediately without even taking time to recall. "Thirty years," she says.

Thirty years. More than half her life. I have mixed feelings as I imagine spending most of my life in this beautiful and yet somehow sterile labyrinth. A blessing or a curse?

The lush oriental rugs under our feet muffle any hint of sound, giving our footsteps a sense of weightlessness. Each turn we take only leads to more hallways, more lavish rooms. Is this a home or a museum?

"The Sterlings have been good to me," Lena continues. "Treated me better than most, I'd say." But there's an odd note in her voice, a hidden complexity, as if beneath the surface there's more she isn't saying.

The deeper we venture into the house, the more signs I see of state-of-the-art smart technology that Nathan Sterling's company is renowned for. Subtle motion sensors are embedded into the plasterwork of the ceiling, the glass walls transition between transparency and opaque with a simple tap, and even the temperature seems to adjust as we move from room to room. The whole house feels alive, like it watches and adjusts to our every movement.

We pass through a grand hall that leads to an impressive library, its walls lined with countless books. I peek in longingly. I know I'm not here for leisurely reading…but as long as I'm living here, surely I will have some down time.

"You like to read?" Lena asks with an approving arch of one pencil-thin eyebrow.

"I do," I admit, my gaze lingering on the room's grandeur. "Books always felt like...friends, you know? They don't leave you." I clear my throat, embarrassed at what I've just let slip.

A faint smile softens Lena's stern features, and for a moment I think she's going to share her own love of reading. But she doesn't comment, simply nods.

"Feel free to read anything you like," she says, "so long as it doesn't leave this room. Mr. Grant's orders."

My heart sinks a little. I imagined curling up in my room with a good book and a cup of hot tea, but it seems that won't happen because of some arbitrary rule whose purpose I can't seem to figure out. Is he worried I'll steal a book? Maybe dog-ear it or spill a drink on it?

Whatever the case, I remind myself that this isn't really my home, even if it will be home for a while. I have to respect the rules—it's the only way I'll last here.

Lena studies me for a few seconds as if waiting to see whether I will push back on this restriction. When she sees I'm not going to, she nods again and points across the room.

"See that door there?" she asks. "That goes into Mr. Sterling's private office. The door is kept locked at all times, but should a mistake be made…" Her voice grew stern, her gaze intent. "You are not to enter that room under any circumstances, you understand?"

"Understood," I say as my eyes follow her pointed finger. I don't know what's behind that door, and it's none of my business. I have no desire to intrude upon anyone's privacy, let alone Nathan Sterling's.

Then again, I wouldn't be half so curious if she hadn't made such an effort to point the door out to me.

Lena holds my gaze for a second longer before offering me a tight smile. "Good," she says. "Even *I* don't go in there, not since the Sterlings moved in."

This only fills my mind with more questions. Before I can contrive a delicate way to ask one of them, however, Lena clears her throat and resumes walking. "I'll introduce you to Mrs. Sterling," she says. "She rarely leaves her room, but if you ever have trouble getting there, remember the house is automated. Just say 'directions to Mrs. Sterling's room' and the house will guide you."

What planet are we on? Should I be excited or deeply troubled by what the housekeeper just said?

Lena heads towards a wide, cream-colored door at the end of the hallway. I follow, looking back once more at Mr. Sterling's mysterious office.

"I trust you have a full understanding of your duties?" Lena asks.

I think back to the online ad that led me here. There were very few details about the exact nature of the help I would be providing, and part of me wonders if the generous pay is in some way buying my discretion. I am equally uncertain why they hired me, a home aide with no experience beyond a few volunteer hours at the local clinic.

"Actually," I say, "I'm not really sure what I'll be doing on a day-to-day basis."

Lena presses her lips together in an expression of…what…disapproval? "I'll give you the rundown," she says. "Mrs. Sterling is physically fit—you won't be helping her to the restroom or feeding her dinner, if that's what you were imagining. Her mind, on the other hand…" Lena trails off, as if following an unspoken thought.

"I'm sorry," I say hesitantly. "What exactly is the matter with her?"

As soon as I say the words, I sense I've overstepped somehow, even though it's a perfectly obvious and natural question.

"I'm sorry if that was indelicate," I say quickly. "I'm just trying to understand how long this is going on and how it started. The better I understand, the better I can—"

"She doesn't go outside this house any more, and rarely leaves her room," Lena interrupts me crisply. "As far as 'understanding'—well, you'll just have to figure her out on your own. I'm not a psychiatrist."

It's clear from her tone that she's done with the topic. I fall silent, puzzled as to why she's not more forthcoming.

We're near the door now. Lena slows her pace.

"The most important thing is keeping track of her medications," she says. "Mrs. Sterling used to handle it herself, but there have been some recent…mishaps. I would take care of it, but I'm too busy running the rest of the house. Even a house as technologically advanced as this one collects dust."

I nod, absorbing her words.

"I will message you a list of her medications," she continues. "Mrs. Sterling takes them every morning at nine, so you won't have to worry about it until tomorrow. It's very important that you actually see her swallow her pills. Going off her medication for even a day could be…catastrophic." A cloud passes over her eyes.

"Anyway," she goes on, clearing her throat, "beyond the medication, it's mostly keeping her company, giving her a sounding board. She can have very strange thoughts sometimes, so it's been decided she ought to have someone on hand who can talk sense into her when necessary."

We've reached the door. I have so many questions, but Lena knocks without waiting for me to speak.

"Mrs. Sterling?" she calls softly. "Emily is here."

As the seconds pass and no answer comes, I can't help asking, "Why did you choose me? I never thought I'd get this job."

Lena looks at me and smiles—I can't tell whether it's a warm smile or a cold one. "I didn't choose you, and if it had been up to me, I would've picked someone much more seasoned. But we all have to work with the hand we're dealt, don't we?"

"Yes," I say, faltering. "I suppose we do."

CHAPTER TWO

I am still working out what to make of Lena's words when a small, timid voice answers from the far side of the door, "Come in."

Lena pushes the door open and I follow her into a bright, sunlit room. The room is filled with lush green plants, their leaves moving gently in the breeze from the open window. The light hits an easel with a half-completed painting on it in the corner of the room. It looks like a landscape, mountains under a crimson sunset, but it's still hard to tell at this stage.

How long has Alicia been living alone in here? When was the last time she and her husband shared the same bed—and whose choice was it to create separate living arrangements?

"Mrs. Sterling," Lena says gently. She's holding my elbow and guiding me forward. "This is Emily Just. She's your new aide."

My eyes land on the figure half-hidden behind a large terrarium at the far side of the room. Alicia Sterling is smaller than I thought she would be. She's wrapped in what looks like a cashmere throw, her hands nervously clutching it around herself as though she is perpetually cold. Her blonde hair is pulled back into a messy bun, a few stray tendrils framing her pale face. Her wide blue eyes look at me, filled with reluctance and a child-like sort of curiosity.

"Hello, Mrs. Sterling," I say.

Alicia gives me a small nod of acknowledgment, her lips pressing into a thin line. It's like she's sizing me up, and for a moment I feel like a specimen under a microscope, scrutinized and judged.

"Please," she says after a beat of uncomfortable silence. "Call me Alicia."

"Alright," I say and then pause, sensing I should say something but not sure what it is. How do you do this, introducing yourself to someone whom you will be working so intimately with? Someone who is so obviously unwell?

I look to Lena for help, but all I see is the door closing behind her. I'm left alone in the room with Alicia, lost in this jungle of green, sunlight, and unease. I swallow hard, tightening my grip on the bag slung over my shoulder. My heart drums a wild beat against my rib cage.

“I’m Emily,” I say much too late, and as soon as the words have left my mouth I feel foolish. Alicia already knows my name—Lena said it when she knocked on the door.

“Lena told me a little about you,” Alicia says. She’s no longer looking at me. Instead her attention is on a nearby fern, studying it intently as if it holds the answers to some unspoken question.

Her voice is soft, almost a whisper. "From a small town, yes? Midwest?"

"Yes," I reply. "Ohio." No need to name the town. I already feel enough like a bumpkin in this state-of-the-art Silicon Valley mansion, dressed as I am in my second-hand thrift store clothes.

Alicia nods, her attention still on the fern. She seems distant, as though she’s somewhere far beyond the walls of this room. I’m hit with a pang of sympathy for her. When did her fear of the outside world begin, and what caused it? What must it be like to remain always indoors, unable to feel the cool kiss of rain or just wander with no sense of purpose or direction?

These are questions I would love to ask her, but of course I can’t do so. They are far too personal, and we’ve only just met.

The silence stretches on, becoming a palpable thing in the room. It's a silence so deep I can hear the gentle hum of the air conditioning and the soft click of a button as Alicia scoops up a tablet and begins tapping at the screen. This house is alive with hidden technology, I realize, a living, breathing entity that seems to pulse with every heartbeat of its inhabitants. The thought both fascinates and terrifies me.

I clear my throat. “So, is there anything you’d like me to do for you?”

Alicia says nothing. She continues to type away at the tablet, and the room subtly changes, the lights dimming, the gentle hum of the air conditioning transitioning into a low thrum of ambient music. Alicia's face is illuminated with an eerie glow, her fingers agile and swift on the screen.

I slip out my phone and glance at the time. Almost two o’clock. Alicia has probably eaten lunch already. Still, better not to make assumptions.

“Are you hungry?” I ask. “I can see if Lena’s got anything in the kitchen.” There is a hint of desperation in my words. I want her to be hungry if only so I’ll have something to do—perhaps that comes with being the daughter of a woman whose answer for every challenge in life was hard work. There are few things more uncomfortable for me than idleness.

"I can't paint when anyone else is in here," Alicia says suddenly. Her attention is still on the tablet even though she's stopped typing. The implication in her words is so blunt that it takes me a few moments to absorb it.

"Of course," I say, recovering myself. "I'll just…" What will I do, wander the house like a lost kitten? Maybe return to the library so I can keep wondering what's in Mr. Sterling's room—and why it's so important that nobody intrude on it?

"I'll see if Lena can use any help," I finish lamely. Alicia offers no response, not so much as a glance, and I find myself wondering how much her social skills have corroded after spending so much time locked away from the world. Or maybe she simply doesn't want me here. After all, Mr. Sterling—Nathan—is the one paying me and presumably the one who picked me.

Did Alicia have any say in the matter?

I slip out of the room as graciously as I can manage, trying not to be stung by the abrupt dismissal.

Still gripping the leather carry bag that contains all my essentials (toiletries, a few changes of clothes, my sleep aid tablets), it occurs to me that Lena never showed me the room where I will be sleeping. While I'm sure there are a great many spare bedrooms in a mansion of this size, the last thing I want to do is make an unfavorable possession by assuming a space that isn't mine. I decide to find Lena and ask her directly about my living arrangements.

I wander the hallways. The mansion seems grander and more labyrinthine with each passing moment. Portraits of past and present Sterlings stare down at me, their sharp gazes making me feel like an invader in a private kingdom. I can't help noticing that for every portrait that bears a resemblance to Alicia, there seem to be three or four that do not—and thus belong to Nathan's ancestry.

They may be husband and wife, but everything about this house tells me it's his child, not theirs.

"Talk about self-indulgent," a voice says, startling me from my thoughts. I turn to see a teenage girl leaning casually against a wall, chewing gum with a defiant air. Her eyes sparkle with mischief, her school uniform askew as though she's just returned from a day of breaking every rule she could find.

“Quite a gallery, isn’t it?” She gestures at the portraits with a sardonic grin. “I told him he should just put mirrors up instead—it would be classier. But Dad likes to do things his own way.”

“Mr. Sterling is your father, then?”

“*Mr.* Sterling,” she repeats with a snort, as if the title itself is a punchline to a private joke I'm not privy to. "The lord of the manor, king of the castle.” Her eyes sweep me up and down, thoroughly unimpressed. “You must be the new girl coming to play nanny to my mom."

"Actually, I'm a home aide." My voice is more defensive than I mean it to be. "But yes, I'm Emily."

"Chloe." She offers no handshake, no welcoming smile. Instead, she dismisses me with a shrug and peels herself from the wall she's leaning against. "Well, Emily the Home Aide, welcome to the madhouse. I’d tell you not to let it swallow you alive, but I guess it’s too late for that.” Her eyes sparkled with something—mischief? Does she know something I don’t, or is she simply having a bit of fun at my expense?

Sensing she’s about to leave, I feel a strange urgency to keep her around, despite her brusque exterior. “Listen, I was looking for Lena. Any idea where she might be?”

“She *might be* just about anywhere,” Chloe says. Other than her dad’s study, I add mentally.

Why do I feel such a strange pull toward Chloe, such a need to win her friendship? Beneath the layers of sarcasm and cynicism, she reminds me of someone—someone I once loved.

The thought drifts away before I can grasp it.

“What do you want with the Nun, anyway?” Chloe asks.

The question throws me for a loop. “The Nun?”

“Lena, the housekeeper. All solemn and dutiful, always following orders, never straying from the righteous path." Chloe's eyes are twinkling now. It's clear that she enjoys ruffling feathers.

"I need to speak with her," I say, trying to keep my tone neutral. "There are certain…details we forgot to iron out.”

Chloe arches an eyebrow, and I decide there’s no harm in explaining.

“I don’t know where I’m supposed to sleep.”

Chloe stares blankly at me for a few seconds. Then her cheeks pull back in a wide grin. "You're joking, right?" she asks, but her grin fades when she sees my serious expression.

"No joke," I say, feeling a familiar heat creeping into my cheeks. "I was...distracted when I first got here. Didn't think to—"

"Oh, this is too good," Chloe interrupts, already laughing. "Emily Just, the home aide who doesn't know where she's supposed to sleep. Priceless."

I feel a flush of embarrassment creeping up my neck and decide it's better to change the topic. "Do you know where I could find her?"

She sighs, still shaking her head at me, and beckons for me to follow. "Come on—I'll show you where you can stay. Best room in the house.

Chloe leads me through a series of winding corridors that seem to twist and turn on themselves. The mansion is far larger than it looked from the outside, with no two rooms alike. She barely looks back to see if I'm keeping up, and I find myself trailing behind her skinny frame, trying desperately not to get lost in this labyrinth of a house.

"Here," Chloe says, halting abruptly in front of an ornate wooden door. The sudden stop nearly makes me collide into her. I steady myself, adjusting my grip on the carry bag. She pushes the door open with a dramatic flourish, and I step forward into the room.

It's spacious, with a high ceiling and wide windows that overlook the rose garden. The decor is lavish, dominated by a large four-poster bed and an antique desk on one side of the room. There's an air of old-world charm here that's offset by an assortment of modern conveniences—an oversized flat-screen television mounted on the wall, an espresso machine on a marble counter near the window, and a sleek, glass-encased shower in the adjoining bathroom. I can't help but admire the view from the window; a riot of colors against an emerald green backdrop. The roses are in full bloom, their vibrant hues standing out starkly against the neat, regimented rows of shrubs and topiaries.

Chloe watches me silently for a moment before her lips curve into a mischievous smirk. "Not too shabby, right?" she quips, crossing her arms over her chest.

"Not shabby at all," I say. If anyone can judge between what is and is not shabby, it's me.

"You get used to it," Chloe says, shrugging.

"But why do they need such a big house?" I ask before I can stop myself. It's an impolite question, and I immediately regret asking. "I'm sorry, I didn't mean—"

Chloe ignores my apology. "It's just my dad's way of showing off, I guess," she says with an indifferent shrug. "Used to have people from his company over all the time, parading them around like he was showing them a new country he'd discovered—or conquered." There is an unmistakable note of disdain in her voice. God knows I went through a rebellious streak in my teenage years…but this seems like more than just bucking against authority.

"Of course," Chloe continues, plopping down on the corner of the bed, "all of that changed when my mom decided the entire world was out to get her." She snorted. Clearly, her disdain was directed toward both her parents, not just her father.

I'd like to ask her more questions, specifically about her mother's condition, but before I can do so she bounces to her feet and heads to the door. "Dinner's at six, but you can eat wherever you want," she says, pausing in the doorway. "Just don't leave dirty dishes around—the Nun has the nose of a bloodhound."

"Thanks, Chloe." Again I feel that strange longing to win her friendship, but it's not until her retreating footsteps have faded down the hall that I realize just whom she reminds me of: Sadie, my best friend through childhood.

And it's no wonder. Sadie was about Chloe's age when she died.

CHAPTER THREE

A disembodied voice pulls me out of a deep sleep. "Miss Just," Lena says, "you are welcome to join us in the dining room for breakfast. If you have any trouble finding the way, the house will guide you, as I said before."

I sit up, embarrassed that Lena should have come into the room and found me in bed...but nobody's around. I'm alone, and the door is closed.

I peer up at the speaker recessed into the ceiling, realizing with a start that Lena is talking to me through the house's communication system. At this point, I shouldn't be surprised, but it's going to take some time to get used to all this fancy technology.

"Coming!" I call. "Just a few minutes!" I don't know whether she can hear me, but I want to do my very best to make a good impression. This is, after all, my first proper day here, and I feel a strange premonition that today will determine how long I stay on here. After all, no contract was signed—if Mr. Sterling changes his mind, he can fire me without a moment's warning.

As I splash water on my face from the slick chrome faucet and clothe myself hurriedly in a pressed white blouse and slacks, I think about last night and the fractured dreams that troubled my sleep. After all the exercise of wandering the house, I felt tired enough not to need my sleeping pills.

But sleeping pills are useful for more things than just sleeping.

After taking one last look in the mirror—essentially just a sleek, black glass panel embedded in the wall—I exit the room, tentatively following the hallway down a spiraling staircase that leads to the first floor. Fortunately, I don't need any house guide: The smell of breakfast cooking provides direction enough.

The dining room is an expansive space, the kind of room I'd only ever seen in movies. It's meant for more than just eating. There are two grand fireplaces on opposing walls, a massive chandelier overhead, a glossy mahogany table that could easily seat twenty, and floor-to-ceiling windows that offer an unobstructed view of the rose garden.

The table is laden with various dishes that make my stomach growl in anticipation. Lena is there, setting up what looks to be a fresh pot of coffee. She turns to look at me as I enter, giving me a curt nod of approval.

"Good morning, Ms. Just," she says, her voice as crisp as the white apron she wears. "You made it down here faster than I expected." Her gaze slips from me to the wall clock and then back to me. It feels like she's silently calculating something.

I'm about to reply when a voice to my left says, "Ah, don't listen to her. She's a machine, that one—all cogs and gears."

I turn to see a man in his late twenties with a mop of dark, rakish hair and a tailored suit jacket over a t-shirt with a picture of a vintage rock band. His eyes hold a glimmer of mischief, but his smile is inviting and warm. "Don't mind Lena—she's been here since forever," he says, pouring a cup of coffee.

He finishes with the coffee and holds it out to me. The gesture surprises me, but I take the coffee and murmur my thanks.

"Trust me," he says in a playful stage whisper, "you're gonna need it around here." He puts out his hand. "I'm Grant, by the way, Nathan's genie-in-a-bottle."

His eyes are filled with a quiet amusement that momentarily eases my nerves. His introduction is unexpected, yet it sends off comfortable sparks of camaraderie. I can see myself being friends with this man, even amidst these alien surroundings.

I grasp his hand, finding comfort in the simple familiarity of human touch in this high-tech fortress. "Emily," I reply, though I'm sure he already knows. "So, what does a genie do around here?"

He chuckles, holding my hand a few seconds longer, then releases me. "Whatever the master commands." He sweeps his arm out, indicating our grandiose surroundings. "Welcome to Sterling Mansion, Emily. It may not be a palace, but it's damn close. But don't let it intimidate you."

It's easier said than done. My eyes take in the enormous picture windows adorned with drapes of opulent silk and the tall marble columns that flank the entrance of a room—a living room, perhaps? I feel even more out-of-place here than I did yesterday, a provincial girl dropped into a world of excess and opulence. My chest tightens, and I take a deep breath, mentally rehearsing an exercise Rich taught me as I try to keep the anxiety at bay.

Grant hands me a plate, then begins stacking his own with breakfast items: a cinnamon roll, several sausages, a handful of bacon, two eggs, buttered toast. It's enough to make a girl wonder how he maintains his figure.

"So," he says as he rearranges the food on his plate to accommodate a scoop of fried potato, "you're Alicia's new friend, huh? Nathan talked about the need for someone to keep Alicia company—she's been in a bit of a downward spiral these past few months, I'm afraid."

It strikes me as odd that he refers to me as a friend rather than hired help. I guess it's an attempt at normalizing the situation, but calling me "Alicia's friend" feels like a disguise I'm donning, hiding the transactional nature of my role here. I wonder if it's part of the Sterling's world, dressing up truths to make them more palatable.

"Friend, caregiver, whatever they need me to be," I answer, trying to sound more confident than I feel. "I'm flexible."

Grant chuckles at that, his gaze briefly flickering to mine. There's a hint of curiosity there that makes me uncomfortable, like he sees through my bravado. "That's a good trait to have around here," he muses before popping a piece of bacon into his mouth.

I fill a bowl with fruit salad and sit opposite Grant. Lena has left the room—she comes and goes like a bat—and it feels very odd to be sitting here, just the two of us at a table laden with enough food to feed a troop of gorillas. I suppose Chloe must have left for school before I came down.

"Is Mr. Sterling not coming to breakfast?" I ask as I spear a piece of honeydew melon.

"Nathan?" Grant finishes his mouthful of toast and chases it down with a swallow of coffee. "No, he takes his breakfast in his office. Likes to get a jump start on the day."

I nod, mulling this over. I have yet to meet the man who hired me, and in truth I know him only through context: his house, his relationships. What am I to make of him? He is clearly very successful in his work…

But at what cost to his family?

A companionable silence fills the room as we both eat. Grant seems to feel no need to break the silence, so I surprise myself by carrying the conversation.

"So," I begin, "how long have you worked for Nathan?"

He too looks surprised for a moment, perhaps having forgotten his earlier comment. Then he wipes his mouth with a napkin and says, "We've worked together for about…oh, sixteen years now. Started right out of college, back when it was more of a family business."

I can't help noticing how he rephrases the question from 'working for' to 'working together.'

"Family business?" I ask.

He waves his hand in a vague gesture, as if it's an irrelevant detail. "Alicia was involved early on, but it didn't last. We all have our different strengths and weaknesses, right?"

I take a sip of coffee, pondering his words. Before I can ask a follow-up question about Alicia's involvement, he hurries on.

"It's been quite the education, let me tell you." He chuckles. "Nathan is a genius—a real genius. Sometimes, it seems like he comes up with a brilliant new idea every quarter hour. It took him some time to develop a thick skin, of course, but he managed."

I raise an eyebrow. "Think skin?"

"Oh, you know how the world is—you have to reach out and take what's yours. It'll never be handed to you. Back in the beginning, Nathan wasn't really ready for this, but he's learned the rules of the game. Doesn't take any shit from anybody now—pardon the French." He shoots me an evaluating look, as if to see whether I'm offended at the curse word. I shake my head to show it doesn't bother me.

"What's the name of his company?" I ask. "I don't think I've heard it."

"AltoTech," Grant replies, dabbing his mouth with a napkin. There's an almost reverential tone when he says the name. "It's a major power player in the tech industry."

I've never heard of it—which doesn't mean much, given my lack of exposure to the tech world. I just press a smile against my lips and nod.

Grant goes on as if I've asked for more information. "Nathan started the company himself," he says. "When he began, all he had was a small loan and a brilliant idea. Now, it's one of the top tech firms worldwide. Had to fight tooth and nail to get recognized, and more than a few competitors learned the hard way that it's better to work with him than against him, but look how it all turned out." He takes a bite from his cinnamon roll and waves it in the air for emphasis.

I can see the admiration he holds for Nathan in his animated retelling of AltoTech's beginnings. To be fair, it is impressive. Not everyone can build such an empire from virtually nothing.

Then again, I can't help wondering how many others' dreams Nathan crushed along the way.

"How much of the technology in this house was designed by him?" I ask.

A cloud passes over Grant's face, and he stops chewing for a moment. Have I overstepped somehow, or am I imagining things?

"Probably most of it," he answers, recovering his formerly relaxed demeanor. "Nathan likes to use his own designs. Especially when it comes to security."

The way he says 'security' makes me uneasy, though I'm not entirely certain why. Despite my better judgment, I find myself saying, "Is all the security really necessary? The cameras, I mean?"

Grant's gaze sharpens, as if he's gauging just how much I've noticed. His mouth tightens into a thin line before he chuckles. "Well, this is more than just a house, it's practically Fort Knox. You'd be surprised how many people want to steal a piece of our success...or to sabotage it."

'Our success.' Was that a slip of the tongue?

I scan the breakfast room again. The polished silverware, the gleaming surfaces—they all seem somehow less inviting now. More like a veneer thinly veiling something darker.

"Besides," he goes on, "there have been a number of break-ins in the area recently. Better safe than sorry, right?"

"Break-ins?" I ask, feigning surprise. God knows it's not the break-ins that make me nervous. It's the idea of being watched all the time, of having my every move recorded and analyzed.

Grant nods. "A few, yes. But no one gets past our security—Nathan makes sure of that. So don't worry. You're quite safe here."

I fight back an urge to shudder. Suddenly I'm not so eager to explore every corner of this house anymore.

Just then Lena—When did she come back into the room, and how much of this conversation has she been listening to?—clears her throat. "Would you like me to prepare a plate for Alicia?" she asks. She is holding one of those pill organizers in her hand, the kind with a separate box for each day.

Glancing at the clock, I realize it's 8:55. I've been so engrossed in speaking with Grant that I've forgotten it's almost time to give Alicia her pills. It wouldn't do to be late on my very first day—I don't know how Alicia feels about punctuality, but it's clear Lena is a stickler for the letter of the law.

And though Lena is only the housekeeper, I get the distinct sense that she—perhaps as much as Nathan—has the power to keep me or dismiss me as she sees fit.

"I'll take care of it," I say, abruptly pushing back my chair and standing. My hip thumps into the table as I do so, and a fork clatters onto the pristine white floor tiles, ringing out in the quiet room. Embarrassment flushes my face. I hastily bend to pick it up.

Graceful, Emily, real graceful.

I can feel Grant's scrutinizing gaze on me, and Lena's too. I'm suddenly hyper-aware of my every movement, as if I'm not just in a high-tech house but on a high-stakes stage. Anxiety gnaws at the edges of my thoughts, yet I take a deep breath and straighten, placing the recovered fork on the table.

I grab a clean plate for Alicia, then pause, my embarrassment deepening. I look to Lena for help.

"Alicia usually prefers a light breakfast," Lena says. "Some fruit, yogurt, and perhaps a piece of toast."

I mutely nod in response, reaching for the bowl of mixed fruits on the table. I spoon a generous serving onto her plate, followed by a dollop of yogurt. After adding a piece of buttered toast to the side, I glance back at Lena for approval.

She nods again, her gaze blank. She hands me the pill organizer, and I take it from her with a murmur of thanks.

I hurry out, sparing one final glance at Lena. Her face tells me all I need to know.

I am on thin ice.

CHAPTER FOUR

As I try my best to find my way back to Alicia's room, I can't help but examine her assortment of pills for the day. There are seven in total: two small white ones, one round blue one, a capsule of some sort, and three others I don't recognize. It's a cocktail of pharmaceuticals that would make any psychiatrist raise an eyebrow.

I suspect a few of these are vitamins, but the rest...what could they be? I check my phone, scanning the text Lena sent me with the names of the medication. From what I can tell, most of these are designed to treat anxiety and depression. Still, it's quite a hefty regimen.

How great must Alicia's fear of the outside world be that she not only never leaves, but she must be doped up on medication all the time? Even as the thought occurs to me, however, I realize that I know what it's like to feel unable to cope with the world, to need a little help to get by. And I also know how quickly you can go from taking something as an occasional relief to depending on it for your day-to-day existence.

But I'm no shrink. It's my job to help Alicia, not to cure her.

To my surprise, I glance to the left and spot Alicia's door. I recognize it because it's the only one that isn't electronic or mechanized. It's an old wooden door, the wood worn and seasoned from years of use. It looks completely out of place in this modern sea of chrome and glass, like a relic from another era.

I give a soft knock before pushing it open gently. "Alicia?" I call out, poking my head in. The room is dim with light seeping through closed blinds, casting horizontal shadows across the floor. A faint scent of lavender lingers in the air—a comforting aroma amidst the sterile atmosphere.

"I brought your breakfast," I announce, pushing the door wider and stepping inside. There she is, lying on a grand canopy bed draped in sheer white curtains, surrounded by a jungle of ferns and flowers and trailing vines. Her eyes are closed, her chest rising and falling rhythmically against the sumptuous velvet bedding. I hear the trickle of water from somewhere, and I can't tell whether it's coming from a fountain or a speaker.

She doesn't respond to my entrance. I don't know if she's asleep or pretending to be, but either way, I don't blame her. I've had plenty of days I didn't wish to face.

I move quietly across the thick carpet, setting down the tray on a polished mahogany nightstand. "It's Emily," I say softly, then immediately feel silly. She's agoraphobic, not senile. I'm pretty sure she remembers who I am.

"Are you awake?" I ask tentatively, half-hoping she doesn't respond so I can escape this room and its oppressive quietude. But Alicia stirs, long lashes fluttering against porcelain skin as her pale blue eyes slowly open. They meet mine with a gaze that is both vacant and piercing all at once—an unsettling combination.

"Yes," she says after what feels like an eternity, her voice soft but steady. "Thank you, Emily."

I nod and back away from the bed, unsure what to do with my hands. Being in her presence is like being near a frightened bird—any sudden movement or loud noise could send her into a state of panic.

She looks at me again, her eyes scanning my face in a way that makes me feel like she's trying to figure me out. "Tell me something about yourself," she says.

The question catches me off-guard. I clear my throat, glancing around the room as if searching for an answer in the cracks of this mostly untouched paradise.

"Well, I guess...I'm from a place called Townsville, Ohio," I start and immediately cringe at how dull that sounds. Why did I share that fact? This is Silicon Valley, the epicenter of innovation and the home of tech giants, and here I am talking about a small, insignificant town in Ohio.

Alicia doesn't seem to mind. "Tell me about Townsville," she says, her gaze never leaving mine as she reaches for her plate. Her interest feels genuine, not the polite kind that people use to fill silence.

"Uh, it's...small," I say, struggling to come up with more adjectives. "Everyone knows everyone else, and there's not much to do except for the annual corn festival and bowling at Lou's Lanes."

She seems intrigued by the mundanity of it all. Or maybe she's just a good actress—I can't tell.

"I mean," I continue, "we don't even have a mall or a cinema. Just one diner, an old library, and a couple of hardware stores. The place is so quiet, you can hear the wind rustling through the cornfields."

A ghost of a smile flits across her lips, as if my words have painted a picture in her mind. "Sounds peaceful."

It's not what I'm expecting. Most people would say it sounds boring. Dead, even. But Alicia seems to appreciate the simplicity, the quietness that my town offers.

"But it's nothing like this place," I add, gesturing to the room around us. Her room with its high-tech gadgets and luxurious décor seems galaxies away from my small-town upbringing.

"No," she agrees, her voice tinged with something that sounds very much like sadness. "It's nothing like this place at all."

We lapse into silence, the room returning to its earlier tranquility. Was that longing in her voice? Does she envy my small-town roots? It is hard to imagine anyone being envious of a life like mine.

She begins poking her pills around. I watch anxiously, recalling Lena's instructions to make sure Alicia takes them all. What was it she said? Missing them for even a day could be 'catastrophic'.

"What about your family?" Alicia asks, breaking me out of my thoughts. She's turned her attention away from her untouched breakfast and back to me.

My heart drops, the subject of family being one I typically avoid. "Well," I start, swallowing the lump that has formed in my throat. "It's just me and my mom now."

Her gaze softens. Why do I have such a hard time concealing my emotions? I feel pathetic, like a lost kitten begging to be adopted.

"What about your father?" she asks.

The question surprises me. She isn't being intrusive—she's just making conversation. I know this, yet her question stirs up a flurry of emotions, memories I'd rather keep buried.

It always comes back to that, doesn't it? The father-shaped hole in my life. Even here, his shadow still chases me.

"He left when I was six," I say, trying to keep my voice steady. Her eyes widen slightly in surprise or sympathy, I can't tell.

"I'm sorry," she murmurs, and I believe her.

"No need," I reply, giving a weak smile. "It's been a long time."

An awkward silence stretches between us. Alicia still hasn't touched her pills. She takes a breath and says, "Well, Emily from Townsville, Ohio, I'd say you're pretty brave—to be here, doing a job like this, far away from home."

"I don't know about brave, more like desperate for a job," I reply with a weak attempt at humor. "I'm trying to save up for my degree."

Alicia's gaze turns serious. "What degree?"

Finally, something I can talk about comfortably. "I want to get my MA in Psychology," I say. "I got my bachelor's, but that was as far as I could get without taking on so much debt I'd be paying it off the rest of my life."

Alicia's eyebrows rise, her eyes reflecting a spark of curiosity. "And what brought you into that field?"

I pause for a moment, contemplating my answer. It's a question I've asked myself over the years. Is it the need to understand my father's abrupt departure or my mother's workaholism? Or am I attempting to decode my own complex maze of insecurities and fears?

"Well," I say after a moment, "I guess...I want to understand people better. Understand why they make certain choices."

She studies me for a moment before nodding slowly as if my answer satisfies her. "That sounds like an admirable goal. I hope Nathan is paying you well."

"He is."

We are both silent, and I sense an opportunity to turn the conversation around. I also sense that we've built some mutual trust, so perhaps I can pry a little more than I would otherwise.

"If you don't mind my asking," I say, "how long has it been since you last went outside?"

Alicia stiffens, her fingers tangling together in her lap. "I don't remember." Her voice is small, her eyes downcast. It's a reaction I've seen in my textbooks—defensive and evasive.

"I'm sorry if I overstepped," I say, feeling a flush of heat rise to my cheeks. "It's just...I want to help you, if possible."

She doesn't look at me as she says, "No need to apologize, Emily." Then she smiles faintly and adds, "You're just doing your job." I detect something in her tone—not reproach, but resignation. She seems tired.

She rises, setting aside the plate. "I'm going to take a walk," she says. "I need to clear my head." She has nearly reached the door when it occurs to me that her pills are all still sitting on her plate.

"Alicia," I say quickly, snatching up the plate. "If you don't mind…"

Alicia gazes down at the plate, and something like disappointment clouds her face. "Ah, yes. I imagine Lena instructed you to make sure you saw me take these. Heaven forbid I should go a single day without medication."

I want to say something, but what? Do I apologize, empathize with her plight? She *is* sick, after all…isn't she?

Alicia reaches out and takes the plate from my hands. With deliberate slowness, keeping her eyes on mine, she pops the pills into her mouth, swallows, and hands me back the empty plate. I watch her walk away, leaving me alone with the uneaten food and my pounding heart.

And the unsettling realization that while she's learned a great deal about me, I've learned very little about her.

Left to my own devices, I decide to tidy up Alicia's room.

I gather the dishes and straighten the pillows on her couch, my gaze lingering over the large windows that offer a panoramic view of sprawling gardens. Everything about the room—the plants, the massive windows—suggests a longing for wilderness and wide-open spaces...and yet this is the private sanctuary of a woman terrified of stepping outside.

As I pick up the discarded wrappers and papers that litter the side table, more thoughts cloud my mind. Surely the Sterlings can afford the best psychologists and therapists. But as far as I can tell, nothing is being done to cure Alicia's condition—only to treat it. She lives in a house that, for all I know, monitors her every word and action, and she's doped up on a regimen of pills that can at best maintain her fragile state of mind, not fix it.

I think back to her earlier words: *Heaven forbid I should go a single day without medication.*

Is this what she wants? Has she chosen this life...or has it been chosen for her?

As I pick up a discarded nightgown, I discover her tablet hidden beneath. To my surprise, the tablet is not password-protected. Stealing a glance over my shoulder to make sure I'm still alone, I open the tablet and begin to navigate its contents. Photos, emails, messages--a digital gateway into Alicia Sterling's world.

Suddenly, I feel a touch of guilt, like I'm peering too closely through a keyhole. What right do I have to pry into Alicia's inner world? Then again, if I'm going to be effective in helping her, I need to know what's really going on, don't I? Isn't that in her best interests?

I come across countless messages from Nathan reiterating his love for Alicia; they seem sincere enough but with an undercurrent of overbearing concern. Emails from different doctors discussing her medication and mental health status flood her inbox. They are mostly unread, from therapists offering different treatment strategies, to wellness clinics inviting Alicia for consultations. It's clear that the world outside is reaching out to Alicia, but she isn't responding.

Then I come across an email from Nathan:

Please, Alicia, you really must give this new doctor a chance. You remember Maimie O'Hagan, the philanthropist we met at that function in LA a few years back? The one with the feather earrings you liked so much?

Anyway, her mother-in-law was a shell of herself after losing her husband. Wouldn't even get out of bed. Then, six months after starting to work with Dr. Harris, she was back at the opera, her spry and happy self once more.

Grant assures me there's no one who understands complex agoraphobic reactive depression better than Dr. Harris. Trust me, if I didn't think he knew what he was talking about, I wouldn't be urging you to work with him. I know it may be a long road to recovery, but it's worth it. We can do this.

Nathan

That email is dated five months ago. Did Alicia give in and start working with Dr. Harris? Has it helped?

Feeling guilty for snooping, I'm about to put the tablet away when I notice a tab at the bottom of the screen—a document Alicia must have left open the last time she was using the tablet. When I pull it up, however, it asks for a password.

The question is, why would there be a password-protected document on a tablet that can be accessed by anyone? And what does the document say?

CHAPTER FIVE

I am wandering through the rose garden when I catch my first glimpse of Nathan.

It is a warm, sunny day—I am quickly getting the impression that every day here is warm and sunny—and the rose garden is a riot of color and perfume. Bees drift lazily among the blooms, and a light breeze carries the scent of roses mixed with the slightly sharper odor of the sea.

When I close my eyes, I imagine I am the only person in the world and all around me is wilderness and beauty, untouched by the hands of man. I am in the ocean of now—no past, no future. Time has stopped. I can remain here forever if I want to, just breathing in the roses and absorbing the sunlight into my skin.

As my feet trace a silent dance across the grass, scarlet blossoms brush against my arm, their thorns catching on the fabric of my blouse. I open my eyes. I am trying to free myself from one particularly tenacious stalk when I hear a soft, deep voice.

"You have to be careful around roses. They are not as delicate as they appear."

I turn, surprised, to find a man I do not recognize leaning against a marble statue nearby. He is a handsome figure dressed in a suit that probably costs more than my annual salary. Coffee-brown hair, slightly mussed as if he's been running his hands through it, frames a deeply tanned face. His eyes, the same oceanic blue as Chloe's, have a striking intensity.

His attention is fixed on the rose in my hand, but he raises his eyes when he senses me looking at him. His gaze is steady and stern and faintly amused.

He hasn't identified himself, but he doesn't need to.

"I'm sorry," I stammer, "I didn't mean to..." Didn't mean to what? Enjoy his rose garden?

"Don't worry about it," he says with a quick shake of his head. He looks comfortable there against the statue, settled in.

How long has he been observing me?

He pushes off from the statue and takes a deep breath. “I have to admit, I thought you'd be older."

"Older?" The remark puzzles me. I just assumed he handpicked me. Did someone else make the decision?

"No offense, Miss Just. I just thought the plan was…" He stops abruptly and dismisses the unspoken words with a wave of his hand as if they are a cloud of gnats. "In any case, the important thing is you're here. I very much hope you can help me get my wife back." He smiles, and I sense genuine affection for Alicia—a worn, frayed affection, perhaps, but affection nonetheless.

"She was my best friend once," he says, his voice laden with nostalgia. "Back when she was still in her right mind. We were partners, teammates…" He sighs. "It's so frustrating, wondering when—if ever—she'll get better. I just want her back."

He sounds so sweetly naïve, like a little boy in need of protecting. My heart stirs, wanting to comfort him…but then I remember how often Dillon put on the same act, used the same disarming vulnerability.

Even after what happened with Sadie.

"I'll do everything I can," I say.

"I trust she's been welcoming?"

"Very much so," I reply, hoping it doesn't sound like an outright lie. The truth is, Alicia hasn’t spoken a word to me since our conversation this morning, and I am beginning to suspect she’s avoiding me. But that’s not information Nathan Sterling needs to know.

He studies me for a moment, his gaze probing. It's like he can see straight through me, straight through my pretenses, and I suspect his words were a test to see whether I'd be honest or defend Alicia.

"I am glad to hear that," he finally says. "She’s a lovely person, but she can be very…irrational.” His words hang in the air between us, and he frowns as if pondering whether to say something more.

"Well, Mr. Sterling," I say, opting not to share my own opinion on his wife’s rationality, "I'm here to do what I can for Alicia. And for your family."

He gives me a brief nod and a small smile—the polite, noncommittal kind. Yet his eyes hold something else, something more profound, like he's taking the measure of me.

"I know you will," he says, and the frown returns. Then, clearing his throat, he says, "Enjoy your walk, Miss Just," and abruptly walks away, leaving me to my thoughts.

If I didn't know better, I might guess I've just spoken with some lonely, eccentric cousin of the family here at the mansion on an extended stay—not the tech mogul Grant spoke so highly of.

Was it all an act? Or is Nathan Sterling a more complicated person than I've given him credit for?

* * *

I find myself lost in the house again, traveling through endless corridors like the lunch settling in my stomach.

The house has a personality of its own. Its vastness, coupled with the ultra-modern, high-tech security features, gives it an omnipresent feel. It watches me from every corner. The walls whisper secrets I yearn to learn, their words muffled by expensive drapery and artwork that hang like elaborate disguises.

Every room I pass is filled with a story. The furniture meticulously arranged and the decorations speak volumes about the lives lived here. It is a grand museum of the Sterlings' existence…and yet I hear more questions than answers, more riddles than revelations.

As I turn down another hallway, I pass a portrait hanging against the wall. It is a family portrait of the Sterlings: Nathan, Alicia, and Chloe. Chloe must be six or seven. The artistry is flawless, each brush stroke detailed to perfection…but why is it so unsettling? Nathan looks happy—triumphant, even. But Alicia…

There's sadness behind her smile—a knowing sadness, like she can predict how everything will play out and she knows it will all turn sour in the end.

A fog of depression settles over me, so I force myself to keep walking. I'm supposed to be keeping Alicia company, helping her to be less lonely, but how am I supposed to do that when she avoids me? Did I fail some kind of test? Has she decided she doesn't like me?

Troubled by these thoughts, I come around a corner and see a bedroom door standing open. Inside can only be Chloe's room, judging by the assortment of grungy band posters on the walls. I hadn't planned to wander into Chloe's domain, but curiosity gets the better of me.

The room is as messy as it is chaotic, a jumble of clothes, loose papers, and random objects piled high. It's the polar opposite of the meticulously organized rooms throughout the house, a clear sign of Chloe's rebellion against her overly-structured life. Despite the mess, there's an undeniable energy in here, an assertion of personality that feels real and raw and refreshing.

At least Chloe isn't pretending.

I hear a toilet flush. Embarrassed, I beat a hasty retreat—but not before a door flies open and Chloe steps out, smoothing her dark hair with a puzzled look on her face. She freezes as she catches sight of me; surprise and annoyance flickers in her eyes.

"What are you doing in my room?" she demands.

"I'm sorry," I say quickly, backing up towards the hall. "I didn't mean to intrude."

She crosses her arms, her gaze hardening as she takes me in. There's defiance there, a challenge. "You think just because my dad hired you, that gives you the right to snoop around? My room is off-limits. Got it?"

"Of course," I stammer, taken aback by her fierce tone. "I...I didn't mean to. It was open and I couldn't find your mother, so…"

This last detail seems to amuse Chloe, and her defiance melts away. She plops herself on the bed. "She's given you the slip, too, huh?"

"Seems like it," I admit, a nervous laugh escaping my lips. "She has a knack for it."

Chloe rolls her eyes, a touch of smirk tugging at the corner of her mouth. "You've got no idea. She might not venture outside, but that doesn't mean she has nowhere to hide if she wants to be alone."

This strikes a chord with me. I know what it's like to disappear, to recede into oneself when reality feels like too much.

A few moments pass in silence, and I begin to feel awkward, standing here uninvited in Chloe's bedroom. "I'll leave you alone," I promise, slowly backing out.

"No, wait," she says unexpectedly, sounding almost regretful. "You don't have to go."

I pause at her words, rooted to the spot by surprise and uncertainty.

She bites her lip, and for the first time, I see a surprising vulnerability in her. She looks younger, a child trapped in a body rocketing toward adulthood.

"It's kind of nice having someone to talk to," she admits. "Lena and Grant don't count."

There's an undercurrent of resentment in her voice when she mentions them, and I can't help but wonder if Chloe is feeling as alienated as I am in this place.

"Okay," I say, returning a few paces. "Well, I guess there's nowhere else I need to be. It doesn't seem like your father has given me many responsibilities."

Chloe laughs. "That's a surprise. He's always been great at delegating—nothing must disturb the great mind at work." Her voice drips with sarcasm.

I sit awkwardly on the edge of her bed, the silence hanging heavy between us. What should I say? I desperately want to win her friendship, to feel like I have at least one ally in this strange new world I've entered, but so far everyone is a walking question mark.

"Your room…" I start, but I'm not sure how to finish. I want to tell her that it feels real, lived-in, unlike the rest of the sterile house. That it reminds me of my old room back in Townsville when I was her age.

"It's a disaster, isn't it?" Chloe interrupts, saving me from fumbling further. She scans her scattered belongings and cracks a self-deprecating smile. "I guess I like it this way. It drives my dad and Lena insane."

I laugh, and for the first time since entering this mansion, I feel a sense of camaraderie. "You should have seen my room growing up," I tell her. "I think you would have found a kindred spirit in me."

Chloe looks at me then, really looks at me, as if she's seeing me for the first time. Not just the hired help, but something more.

A friend, perhaps?

"You can tell a lot about a person from the state of their bedroom," I continue in a lighter tone, hoping to build on our tentative rapport. "Like how if it's too clean, it can suggest they're hiding something."

Chloe chuckles and nudges a crumpled shirt on the floor with her foot. "Guess I'm an open book then."

I glance around the room again, taking in the posters on the wall—bands I've never heard of—and the stack of scribbled notebooks on her desk. "What's all this?" I ask, gesturing towards them.

"Oh, those?" Chloe glances at the pile before shrugging nonchalantly. "Just some stuff I write... songs, poems. Random thoughts, mostly," she says, her voice trailing away.

"Would you mind if I..." I gesture to the notebooks, asking for permission without needing to elaborate further.

Chloe eyes me warily for a second before shrugging again, "Knock yourself out."

I gingerly pick up the topmost notebook and flip it open. The first page greets me with a rush of nostalgia, the ink-smeared letters and chaotic doodles reminding me of my teenage journals. It feels intimate and intrusive all at once.

I read a few lines aloud. "Silent halls echo voices long gone...eternal spectators of ghostly laughter. A home once lived, now a monument of past fractures."

Chloe's eyes meet mine, a flicker of surprise crossing her face as she leans back against her bedpost. I close the notebook gently, placing it back on the stack.

"You're very talented," I say sincerely, trying to convey the depth of my admiration for her words.

A reddish hue colors Chloe's cheeks and she quickly looks away, her fingers drumming a nervous rhythm against her leg.

"Tell that to my dad," she mutters, avoiding my gaze.

"Why wouldn't your father appreciate your writing?" I ask, my curiosity getting the better of me.

Chloe shrugs again. "He thinks it's a waste of time. Says I should be focusing on more 'important' things, such as getting prepared for college. I asked him if he thought I should apply to the writing course at Cal State. He was like, 'You can go wherever you want, honey.' He hasn't read anything I've written, I know that. Guess he's too busy managing his empire."

I remember my own mother's busyness, working multiple jobs, and how invisible I'd felt much of the time. "Parents can be hard to please," I say, hoping to share some common ground.

"Is your dad the same way?"

For a moment, I'm at a loss for words, caught off guard by the unexpected question. "My dad...he left when I was young," I admit, looking down at my hands.

Chloe shifts awkwardly, her previous bravado replaced by a sudden discomfort. "Oh, I'm...I'm sorry, Emily," she stammers, and I can't help but feel a pang of regret for having inadvertently dampened the mood.

"No, it's okay," I assure her quickly. My past is what it is, and though it's painful to dig up, it's also a part of me. A part of who I am. "You didn't know."

We sit in silence for a moment, the previous lightheartedness gone, replaced by a mutual understanding of parental disappointment and the burden of carrying unmet expectations. I can certainly see the root of Chloe's disdain for her father—he is all about structure and control, and it's completely understandable why a teenage girl would naturally buck against that.

Then I think of her comment about her mother suddenly deciding that all the world was out to get her. It struck me as an unfair characterization at the time. Is it simply a teenager's resentment for her mother's condition, or is it based on something more tangible, something I don't know about? I feel an urge to delve deeper into this, but I can't just ask outright. It's Chloe's story to share, not mine to pry.

We lapse back into silence, each lost in our own thoughts. The room feels different now, charged with shared confidences and the echo of unspoken words. I don't wish to ruin the fragile friendship we've formed, so I decide to make my exit.

"I should probably get going," I say eventually, rising from my seat. "I still have a lot to learn about this place."

She nods in understanding, looking a little relieved. "It was nice talking, Emily."

"I enjoyed it too, Chloe."

"Are you going to be at the party tomorrow?"

I frown—this is the first I've heard of it. "What party?"

"It's a silly thing the neighborhood does—every month, they hold a party at a different house. Tomorrow's our turn." She rolls her eyes, making it clear what she thinks about this idea.

I'm not sure what to make of this news. The idea of having a party here—as in bringing a group of people into the home of a woman as inhibited as Alicia—seems almost cruel. Then again, perhaps she likes having company.

And if she doesn't, she can always stay in her room, can't she?

"Yes," I answer. "I don't really have anywhere else to be, do I?"

Chloe smiles. "I guess not."

I leave her room feeling strangely lighter than when I entered, as if sharing my past with Chloe lifted some of the weight off my shoulders. A part of me wonders if she felt the same way.

Maybe I'm not so alone here, after all.

CHAPTER SIX

The next afternoon, as I grasp the handle of the door leading into Alicia's room, I am surprised to find it locked. It wasn't locked when I served Alicia breakfast this morning...so why is it locked now?

The party is about to start, and I thought I would come and see if Alicia wants to join everyone. Seeing new faces, or at least faces she hasn't seen in a while, could be good for her, and it would give others a chance to see she's doing okay. Finding the door locked troubles me, and I have to keep myself from imagining the worst.

"Alicia?" I knock lightly on the polished oak door, trying to keep my voice calm and unimposing. "It's Emily. May I come in?"

Silence.

I wait for a few moments, hoping that maybe she's just taking a while to get to the door. But as the seconds drag on, it becomes increasingly clear that she's not coming to the door.

A cold, clammy fear sets in. What if she has done something to herself? Anxiety and depression are cousins, and I know too well how such dark thoughts can consume a person. I take a deep breath, trying to keep my rampant imagination in check.

"Alicia, I'm getting really worried about you." I press my ear to the door and listen for any sounds.

The silence is deafening.

"Okay," I murmur to myself, stepping back. "Think it through, Emily." I have no illusions about being able to break down the door, pick the lock, or otherwise force my way in. That leaves only one option: Get help. In the back of my mind I'm dimly aware of all the cameras positioned throughout the house, and though I know Nathan must be monitoring his wife's bedroom as well, there's a good chance he's distracted with the party.

Just a few minutes ago, I heard him asking Grant for his feedback on a speech he was planning as I passed them in the hallway. I get the distinct impression that a neighborhood get-to-together isn't just a social event in Nathan's world. It's a chance for him to further cement his image: the gracious host, the successful tech mogul, the doting husband.

Shoving these thoughts aside, I race down the hallway. I don't have any clear sense of direction, however, and so I am quickly lost, wandering through the labyrinthine mansion looking for help. The house seems even more intimidating than it did when I first stepped inside, its sprawling corridors stretching out before me like a maze.

As I sprint around a corner, I nearly collide with Lena. She looks taken aback as I skid to a halt inches away from her, her eyes wide with fright. In her arms, she's holding a tray laden with silver goblets and an expensive-looking bottle of champagne.

"Emily," Lena gasps, one hand clutching her chest as if to steady herself. "You nearly gave me a heart attack! What's the matter?"

"It's Alicia," I blurt out. "She's locked herself in her room!"

Lena's eyes narrow, the surprise transforming into something more like suspicion. "Have you tried knocking?"

"Of course!" I say, exasperated. "I called her, too, but she didn't answer."

"Maybe she's sleeping. She sometimes takes naps in the afternoon and doesn't like to be disturbed. Probably timed it carefully, too."

It takes me a moment to understand the implication. "You think she's just trying to avoid the party? But what if it's something more serious?"

Lena arches an eyebrow. "Such as…?"

"What if she's hurt? Or worse?"

Lena looks at me for a long moment, her eyes hard and assessing as they bore into mine. "And what makes you think that might be the case? Do you have any reason to believe she would do something?"

It is only the third day since I arrived here, so I really haven't had much time to gather evidence. I search through my memory but can't find anything solid to substantiate my concern.

Still, if anything happened to her and I did nothing about it…

Lena, watching me closely, lets out a sigh. "If you ever hear her talk about suicide or harming herself, you must inform me right away. Otherwise, we have no reason to believe she would take such drastic measures."

"Has she ever hurt herself before?" I ask.

Lena gives me a sidelong look and adjusts the grip on the tray. "The guests are about to arrive, and we still don't have enough serving utensils in the dining room. Would you mind helping me set things up? I promise I'll ask Nathan about Alicia as soon as I get a chance."

I chew my lip, hating the idea of just leaving Alicia to her own devices. And why did Lena ignore my question? Doesn't she realize that if Alicia has a history of self-harm or suicide, I need to know about it in order to be on the lookout for similar behaviors?

"Alicia is a grown woman," Lena says. "She can take care of herself. And if you want to stay on her—to save up for that master's degree, is that right?—you'll learn to respect the way things are done." There is no mistaking the veiled threat in her words.

"Now," she says, smiling thinly, "about those serving utensils."

Feeling trapped and thoroughly out of my element, I drop my head and follow her.

* * *

The party is in full swing by the time we finish setting up the dining room. Nathan is surrounded by a group of admirers, all hanging onto his every word. He's holding court, delivering some anecdote that has everyone in stitches. Grant Davis is lurking at the edge of the group, his enigmatic eyes scanning the crowd before they land on me.

I feel my cheeks heat up under his gaze, and I quickly busy myself with refilling champagne glasses. I'm a caregiver, not a server, but Lena has made it clear there's no place for arguing when it comes to the Sterling household. Besides, I can't shake off my gagging worry about Alicia. I wonder if Nathan even cares that his wife is missing from their gathering.

Lena has gotten pulled into a conversation. She looks oddly relaxed, laughing as she tells some story or other about something silly Chloe did when she was a child. It's a side of Lena I've never seen before, and it makes me question my conclusions about her stony nature.

Is it possible her stern stoicism is no more than a front?

Still pondering this, my gaze lands on Chloe. She's standing near the French windows, her silhouette visible against the twilight outside as she scrolls her phone, worlds away from the party going on around her. She looks so much like Sadie, my heart aches.

I'm about to make my way to Chloe when a loud voice at my elbow says, "So you must be the new aide Nathan was talking about."

I turn to see a short man with wire-framed glasses and what can only be described as an 'enthusiastic' hairstyle involving several tufts of white hair sticking out haphazardly in all directions. His eyes twinkle behind the lenses, emanating an energy that feels sorely out of place in the somber Sterling household. His beard bristles in all directions.

It occurs to me that he's the neighbor I waved to just after arriving here—the one who didn't wave back.

"Yes, I'm Emily," I reply, extending a hand.

"Marcus Welby," he says, shaking my hand with gusto. "Nice to finally meet you, Emily. Heard a lot about you, I must say." His eyes twinkle with an insatiable curiosity, and I get the impression that he has forgotten our earlier encounter. "You're one brave lady to take on the task. Alicia isn't known for being exactly...accommodating. And Nathan's got enough walls around him for a fortress."

His words strike me as intrusive and over-familiar, given that we've just met. But there's something about Marcus that makes me feel as if I can trust him, despite the underlying sense of unease his words stir up. Perhaps when I encountered him before, he was simply in a mental fog.

"I'm just grateful to have the job," I say, trying to be diplomatic.

He chuckles, eyeing me with an amused grin. "I'm sure. But trust me, Emily, there's more to this job than meets the eye." Still smiling, he leans close and murmurs, "All is not as it seems."

I frown, taken aback by this unexpected insight. Marcus goes on as if nothing happened.

"Don't be charmed by the dashing genius, the sassy daughter, the mad wife," he says with a polite smile at odds with the nature of his words. "It's all a show—trust me. At the heart of this company is a ruthless monster who will crush everything in his path to get what he wants."

An older couple, each carrying a champagne glass, pass by, and Marcus smiles and nods at them. I try to smile as well, but I am puzzled by Marcus's words. Why is he telling me all this, and what does it mean?

"You may not know this," he says, "but I was one of the company's first investors. I've known the family for over twenty years, had a first-row-seat to the rise of AltoTech." His nostalgic smiles seems to freeze. "Back when it was Nathan and Alicia making the decisions, I felt comfortable with the direction of things. But now..." He trails off, momentarily lost in memory. "Now I wouldn't touch this company with a ten-foot pole."

His words remind me of something Grant said the other day about Nathan's competitors learning that it was better to work with him than against him. How many careers, how many lives, has Nathan ruined in his quest for power?

Should Alicia's name be on that list, too?

Marcus clears his throat and smiles. "Listen to me, prattling on about ancient history! I should show you around the area next time you have a day off if they don't work you into the ground here. It's quite a lovely part of the country."

"That sounds nice," I say, feeling whiplash at the sudden change in tone.

He pulls out his phone and passes it to me. For a moment, I can only stare, puzzled.

"Your number," he says. "So we can stay in touch."

I don't particularly want to give him my number, but I feel too embarrassed to turn him down now—not to mention that I can't think of a suitable excuse. Besides, maybe it would be good to have someone to reach out to.

Hiding my reluctance as best I can, I smile and enter my number into his phone before passing it back to him.

"You'll love the area," he says, returning the phone to his pockets. "The museums, the preserves..." He trails off, his gaze focused on something behind me.

"Well, well, there's Nathan himself!" he says. "I should go say hello. Catch up with you later, Emily," he says, already stepping away.

So there I stand, champagne glass in hand, left wondering what to make of the bizarre encounter.

Is he just an eccentric old man? Is he paranoid?

Or should I take his warnings to heart?

CHAPTER SEVEN

I am corralling a few stray hairs, sweeping them back from my forehead and tucking them behind my ear, when Rich appears on the screen. His face is blank for a second, then brightens with a warm smile as he sees me.

"Good to see you, Emily. How's the California air treating you?"

It's eleven a.m., the day after the party, and Alicia is in a therapy session of her own with Dr. Raymond Harris. I figured I might as well schedule my own appointment for the same time slot—it's not as if I have any other duties to take care of at the moment.

I am sitting out in the rose garden, lost amidst the tall stalks and the velvety fragrance of the flowers. I didn't want to risk being recorded during my session with Rich, so I opted to go outside instead.

"Breezy," I reply, matching Rich's grin. He's always had a way of making me feel at ease despite the professional boundary between us. "I can't exactly say it's much different given that I hardly step outside the mansion."

Rich chuckles and leans back in his chair, studying my face. "How are you settling in?"

"Fine," I say, trying to sound convincing. "The Sterlings...they're an interesting bunch."

He tilts his head to one side, concern etched on his features. "Interesting how?"

"Well…" I hesitate for a moment, unsure of how much truth to spill. The Sterlings, for all their wealth and glamor, exude an aura of intense secrecy. Living in their mansion feels like tiptoeing around a minefield, always on high alert for the unknown.

"There's a tension in the house," I finally say.

"Elaborate," Rich says.

"It's like everyone is hiding something. Like they're all players in a game that I've yet to understand. Even Marcus Welby, the neighbor, gave me an odd warning last night. About...about not trusting anyone until I knew what they wanted."

Rich raises his eyebrow at this. "Do you feel unsafe, Emily?"

I chew my lip nervously. "I wouldn't say unsafe. Just...unsettled, maybe. Like I'm making my way across a lake, and I keep hearing the ice creak beneath me."

“That sounds unsafe to me.”

I shake my head, unsure how to say what I mean. The last thing I want is for him to become convinced I’m in danger—I need this job too much.

"I think it's more a matter of adjusting," I explain. "To the massive house, the high-tech security...their strange family dynamics. It's all just...alien to me."

Rich studies me. I sense he’s unconvinced, but he doesn’t say anything. This is one of his tactics—sweating me out.

“When was the last time you left the house?” he finally asks.

I shrug one shoulder. “I’m out in the rose garden right now.”

He shakes his head. “I mean leave the property. Really get away.”

“Not since I arrived.”

“It’s been four days, Emily. You told me you’d be right next to the Pacific.”

“I am—I can see it from one of the windows in my room.”

“But you haven’t been to visit?”

I lift my hands and drop them, flustered. “I’m just…it’s busy, you know? So much to do, to learn. We had a party just yesterday. And Alicia—she’s unpredictable. Never know what a day’s going to be like with her.”

I’m babbling now, and I can tell Rich sees it, too.

He holds up a hand, effectively silencing me. "Deep breath, Emily. You're safe to speak here. Always remember that."

I nod reluctantly, squeezing my hands together in my lap. My fingers feel clammy, and I swallow hard.

"It's just...overwhelming," I admit sheepishly. "So different from what I'm used to back home."

Rich nods sympathetically. "It's a big change, no doubt. But that’s why it’s especially important for you to take care of yourself. You're in a new environment, dealing with high-pressure situations. It's important to have some time for yourself, some breathing space."

I sigh, knowing he's right. "I'll try, Rich. I just...I need this job, okay? I can't afford to mess this up."

“Your mental health is more important than this job,” he says gently.

I nod, knowing he's right—but my mental health isn't only tied to day-to-day events here. It's also tied to my future, my goals. If I lose this job, that will be a huge setback for me, and I can already imagine the depression that will crush me like an avalanche. So, I would argue it's very much in the best interest of my mental health to keep this job at all costs.

But Rich will probably find a clever way to poke holes in my perspective, so I keep this to myself.

Rich waits, watching me intently. I have to give him something.

"It just seems unfair," I say. "Going outside, exploring the Pacific, when I know Alicia is trapped here in her huge, gilded cage. It's like I'm mocking her freedom."

Rich tilts his head to the side, a knowing look in his eyes. "But you're not Alicia, are you, Emily?"

"No," I admit quietly. "I'm not."

"And your freedom isn't contingent on hers." He leans forward in his seat. "Don't imprison yourself because of someone else's situation."

I blink, a dull ache forming at the back of my skull as I process his words. Is that what I've been doing? Internally mirroring Alicia's confinement?

A butterfly drifts past me, its wings a blur of orange and black. It circles the blooming roses once before flitting away, lost amidst the verdant maze of the garden. For some reason, this momentary visitor wrenches my heart. It reminds me of what I am not—an innocent creature unfettered by the ghosts of the past, unburdened by anxiety and self-doubt.

I glance at the screen, but it's frozen—I must have lost my Wi-Fi connection. "Hold on, Rich," I say as I pick up the laptop and stand. "I'll call you back in just a minute."

I close the laptop and hurry toward the house, the clipped grass cool beneath my bare feet. As I reach the huge glass doors of the mansion's side entrance, I pause, glancing back at the garden one last time. The butterfly has vanished, leaving me alone with my thoughts.

The mansion is as silent as a tomb when I enter. The air is cool and artificial as it hits my face. Any semblance of warmth or life is meticulously regulated by the state-of-the-art technology Nathan has installed.

Having wandered the house for most of four days now, I am beginning to get my bearings. I head straight for my bedroom. I don't relish the idea of continuing the counseling session inside the house, but perhaps I can keep the conversation away from any topics that might get me fired, such as discussing my growing concerns about Nathan's treatment of his wife.

I hurry down a hallway, passing the door to Alicia's room. As I do so, I am surprised to see Lena standing there. She straightens immediately, but I have no doubt that just a few seconds ago she had her ear pressed to the door.

"Oh," I say, coming to an abrupt stop. "Is Alicia's session over already?"

Lena looks flustered. "No, I just...I thought I heard something, a noise." She clears her throat, brushing invisible dust off her apron. "It was probably nothing."

I narrow my eyes slightly, though Lena avoids meeting my gaze. I've never seen her look this uncomfortable before. She is normally so composed and aloof, almost indifferent. To my surprise, anger flares up in me at the knowledge of what she's been doing.

How much of Alicia's confidential conversation has Lena—the housekeeper, for goodness' sake—overheard?

"I thought the cameras recorded everything," I say. "I didn't realize you did, too."

At this, her face turns red—not with embarrassment, but with rage. Or perhaps a combination of the two. She rushes toward me, and for a moment I think she's going to slap me. I almost raise the laptop in self-defense.

But she pulls up, pointing a crooked finger at my face. "You mind your own business, Emily Just," she hisses. "You've no idea what goes on in this house." A tremor passes through her hands, but her gaze is steely. "And you'd do well to remember that."

We are both breathing heavily, staring at one another like a pair of winded bulls. I am not usually one for confrontation, but this brazen invasion of Alicia's privacy—preying on a woman whose mind is already preying on itself—strikes me as both cowardly and cruel, and I can't just back down.

Not even if my job depends on it, as it very well may.

Before I can say something I may regret, however, the door opens and Dr. Raymond Harris steps out. He is a tall, lean man with salt-and-pepper hair combed neatly to the side. His glasses are perched precariously on his hawkish nose, giving him an intellectual look.

"Everything alright here?" he asks, his scrutinizing gaze darting between Lena and me.

Lena clears her throat, quickly regaining her composure. "Yes, everything's fine," she says. "There was just a...misunderstanding." She shoots me a glare, as if daring me to contradict her, but the entrance of a third party has cooled some of my anger. Catching Lena eavesdropping is a valuable card to have—perhaps even more valuable in reserve than if I played it.

I put on the best smile I can manage. “Thank you for the clarification, Mrs. Brooks. I’ll keep what you said in mind in the future.” I nod at Dr. Harris and then hurry off down the hallway, a single question burning in my mind.

Is Lena as much a spy for Nathan as the cameras scattered throughout this house?

CHAPTER EIGHT

After finishing my session with Rich, during which I carefully avoided describing the interaction with Lena outside Alicia's room, I wander into the library, hoping to find something to ground my restless mind.

If my conscience won't let me escape the property physically, maybe I can escape another way.

As my fingers trail along the spines of the books, I recall all the times I sat on the floor of my room as a child, paging through one of my picture books while my parents' angry words filled the house. The house back in Townville is much smaller than the Sterlings', and the walls are so thin that even the quietest whispers can be clearly heard from the other side. I'd burrow between the pages of my books, using the stories to drown out the reality just outside my bedroom door.

Now here I am in a mansion far removed from that small Ohio home, but I find myself in the same predicament: trying to ignore the unsettling events surrounding me and seeking solace in books.

I pull out a worn, leather-bound book with gilt-edged pages: *Wuthering Heights*, a story known for its twisted love and haunting ghost stories. Fitting, I muse, as I carry it over to a plush leather armchair by the window, where the rain splatters against the glass in a somber rhythm. I sink into the leather, the smell of old books and polished oak wrapping around me like a comforting blanket.

I open to the first page and try to lose myself in the words.

No matter how carefully I read, however, the words are just words—they carry no deeper meaning, draw no pictures. Instead, my mind keeps going back to those remembered arguments, the sharp edges of my parents' words as they shouted at each other for hours. "How am I supposed to work all day and then come home to a place like this?" my dad would say, and my mom would answer, "Maybe if you had a real job, we would have a real home."

It's strange, remembering those fights. They were so bitter, and yet I also feel a sense of nostalgia. After all, I still had two parents back then. My dad may have taken the fights with him when he left for good when I was just six years old…but maybe it would've been better to have a father around, even if all they did was fight.

I guess that's something I'll never know.

My gaze shifts from the book to the rain-soaked window, where I find my own reflection staring back at me, distorted and hazy. The lines of worry etched on my forehead seem darker, deeper, under the stormy lighting. I can't help but wonder if this job, helping Alicia Sterling, was a mistake.

Alicia's mind isn't the only fragile one in this house.

Just then, the door at the other end of the library—the door to Nathan's forbidden office—opens and laughter spills out. A woman is standing there beside Nathan, his hand resting on her hip. She is short and petite with long, charcoal, perfectly-straight hair to go with her perfectly-straight teeth, which seem to glow in the soft lighting inside the office.

"Until next time," the woman says, and Nathan's hand slips away. Unaware of my presence, she crosses the library in high heels, her head bent and a private smile lingering on her face. She notices me and pulls up abruptly, placing a hand on her chest.

"Oh. I didn't see you there."

I am about to introduce myself, but she hurries past me without another word—too busy, it seems, for such trivialities as introductions.

For a moment I sit there in stunned silence, the book in my lap forgotten. Who was that woman? Was she just a colleague, a business partner? Or was she something more? The sight of his hand on her hip flashes before my eyes again, and a knot forms in my stomach.

I glance towards Nathan's office, but the door is closed now. It's just as well—I wouldn't expect to get any truthful answers from Nathan himself.

With a sigh, I pick up my book again and try to refocus my attention on the words. I am even more distracted than before, however, so I close the book and return it to the shelf. I don't know what I plan to do, but I have to do something. Sitting here is driving me crazy.

I leave the library and begin walking with no sense of direction, passing paintings and portraits of past Sterlings in ornate frames. Each one seems to be watching me, their eyes following my every move—much like the cameras sprinkled through this building may be doing, as well.

Never have I felt so paranoid—and never have I had so much reason to feel paranoid.

I become aware of the sound of footfalls behind me. At first I think I'm imagining it, but no, it's real. Someone is following me—or simply going the same way I'm going, I can't tell.

I pick up my pace, not daring to look back. I imagine Nathan striding toward me, his face tight with anger, ready to give me a piece of his mind for sticking my nose where it doesn't belong. Only…what did I do but read a book in the library? I wasn't spying on anyone. That's Lena's MO, not mine.

The footsteps get louder. "Emily! Wait, Emily!" Is that Nathan's voice? I can't quite tell, and suddenly I'm on the verge of panic. He's going to fire me, to tell me I'm more trouble than I'm worth, and all of this will have been for nothing. Forget earning my master's, forget helping Alicia—I'll be thrown out like a bouquet of dead roses, here today and gone tomorrow.

The fears spiral faster and faster like a circling cloud of bats, descending on me until all I can hear is the frantic beating of their wings filling me ears, filling my head, and I race forward to escape the noise, running for all I'm worth—

And then a hand grabs my arm, jerking me to a stop.

"Emily!"

I turn to see Grant staring at me with a look of stunned concern. His stormy gray eyes are wide, eyebrows slightly furrowed as if he can't figure out why I was running.

"Grant," I say, relief washing over me like a cold shower. It's not Nathan. I'm not getting fired. The bats scatter, and I'm standing in an empty hall with Grant Davis, panting like I've just finished a marathon.

He lets go of my arm, visibly relaxing. "You okay?" His voice is calm and collected, the complete opposite of how I feel right now.

"I...I thought..." I shake my head, unsure how to explain what I mean.

"You'd better sit down before you fall," Grant says, leading me to a plush velvet bench nestled in an alcove. I sink onto it, pressing my clammy hands to my face as I try to calm my racing heart. It feels like it's trying to beat its way out of my chest.

Grant crouches down in front of me, his expression earnest. "Now tell me. What's going on? Why did you run from me like that?"

"I don't know…" I swallow hard, trying to compose myself. "I was in the library, reading a book, and the door to Nathan's office opened. He was there with another woman—not Alicia—and I thought if he knew I'd seen them together like that…if he knew what I knew…"

Grant's smile is full of relief. "You're talking about Rebecca Chen. She's Nathan's business partner—they were likely in a meeting."

"Likely?" I ask, puzzled that Nathan's right-hand man wouldn't know for certain.

Grant shrugs. "I may be his assistant, but that doesn't mean I know every detail of his waking life."

I press my lips together doubtfully, wondering if I should say anything more or keep silent.

Grant lowers his face to draw my eyes to his. "Is there something more you need to tell me?"

"It's just…" I hesitate, and then the words spill out in a rush. "The way he had his hand on her hip, it just seemed so personal, so intimate. And then I felt guilty for having seen it—but it's not like I'm going to tell anyone, am I? Other than you." I'm blushing. Might as well cut my losses and shut up.

Grant smiles and squeezes my hand. His hand is warm, smooth, and much larger than mine. "Nathan's always had a thing for Rebecca. They flirt a little, light up when they see one another, but it's harmless. They're both married, and they're both too smart to complicate their lives with an affair. Besides, I'd know if something more was going on—I keep a close eye on things." He winks at me.

His words, so full of certainty, reassure me and I find myself nodding. "I wasn't trying to see anything I shouldn't," I say. "Honestly."

"I believe you." He pauses, thinking. "Has Lena gotten you all stirred up?"

I chew my lip, thinking of the incident between us outside Alicia's room. I don't want to talk about it, because that will inevitably lead to what started it—catching Lena spying on Alicia during her session with Dr. Harris. And there's no telling what might happen if I share *that* little detail with Grant.

"She has, hasn't she?" Grant says, nodding to himself. "I'll have a talk with her, remind her of her place. She needs that now and then."

Still, I say nothing. As much as I appreciate him going to bat for me, I don't want to give the impression that I asked him to do it. I don't need Lena to be my enemy any more than she already is.

Grant straightens and finally pulls his hand away from mine. "Now, I want you to stay here a few more minutes, okay? Deep breaths. And when you're feeling better, get outside. When was the last time you went to the ocean?"

The question surprises me—Rich asked me about the ocean, too.

"I've…never been to the Pacific Ocean, actually."

He shakes his head in wonder. "You are a marvel, Emily Just. Well, if you need a ride, you can always borrow my car. Or we could go together—might make for a fun afternoon." He adds this like an afterthought, but I can't help but get the impression it's been on his mind for a while.

I smile. "Sounds lovely."

He smiles back. "Tomorrow afternoon? Say…four o'clock?"

I don't like making decisions so quickly, but given how kind he's been to me—not to mention the prospect of getting to see the Pacific up close for the first time—I can't help but nod. "Four o'clock works."

"Good. See you then." He flashes another smile and then hurries off, leaving me to the silence of the house.

It seems, then, I have two allies here: Grant and Chloe. They have their secrets too, I am sure, just I have mine. But at least I can trust their intentions.

As I practice taking deep breaths, I think over Grant's words about the relationship between Nathan and Rebecca. Maybe he's right, and it's just a bit of harmless flirting. Considering how depressed and withdrawn Alicia is, it's understandable that her husband would be desperate for companionship.

And yet I can't help wondering if I've gotten the cart before the horse—if perhaps Nathan isn't seeking companionship elsewhere because his wife is agoraphobic, but rather Alicia is agoraphobic because Nathan is seeking companionship elsewhere.

Doping her up on medication, monitoring her every word and action, spying on her therapy sessions—what better way to control her and keep her from creating any ripples in the perfect life Nathan has created for himself?

CHAPTER NINE

All through the rest of that day, while I busy myself about the house with whatever chores I can find, I think about Grant's invitation and wonder if it was a mistake to agree.

In retrospect, going to the ocean together, just the two of us, sounds very much like a date—and I hardly even know the guy. But what was I supposed to say, being put on the spot like that? I guess I could've asked for more time, but it's a lot easier to think of that in retrospect than in the moment.

Maybe it'll be fun. Rich made it clear I need a break from this house, and a trip out could be a welcome distraction. Plus, it's not like I've any other plans. The Sterling mansion isn't exactly overflowing with social opportunities.

I find myself in Alicia's room again, as I have so often since starting this job. It's dim, the only light coming from the soft glow of her tablet screen. She's huddled underneath her blankets, her eyes wide and unblinking as she stares at the device in front of her. I glance around but find no sign of anyone else. No surprise there.

"Hey, Alicia," I say softly, approaching the bed. "Need anything?"

"No," she mumbles without looking up from the tablet. When I entered the room, she was busily tapping away at the screen, but her fingers have gone still since then. She told me she can't paint with anyone else around, and maybe she can't write unless she's alone, either.

But what is she writing? Does it have something to do with that password-protected document I found on her tablet the other day?

"Alright," I say, trying not to take her dismissal personally. "I think I'll just tidy things up a bit if you don't mind. Gives me something to do."

No answer. I set to work.

As I move around the room, picking up discarded clothes and straightening crumpled papers, my mind wanders back to the implications of Nathan's relationship with Rebecca. Is Alicia aware of their closeness? If so, how does she feel about it? Does she realize the extent to which she's been controlled?

As much as I wish to broach the subject with her, I'm too worried about what might happen. She could panic, go into hysterics, and then I'll have to explain what happened.

Besides, Nathan may be listening to our every word. If I want a private conversation with Alicia, I'll need to speak with her somewhere more secluded—which is quite a conundrum, considering her unwillingness to leave the house.

Perhaps there are places inside that house where we can speak privately, though. Chloe might know. I make a mental note to ask her as discreetly as I can.

While I'm reaching for a tissue that fell behind a fern, Alicia crawls out of bed and heads to the bathroom, leaving her tablet on the edge of the bed. As the door shuts behind her, I find myself drawn to the screen.

How long will Alicia take in the bathroom? A few minutes?

I don't like snooping—there's a reason I got so heated when I caught Elena eavesdropping on Alicia's therapy session. But there's a crucial difference between Elena's snooping and mine: I have Alicia's best interests in mind.

Tossing the tissue into a waste basket, I move closer to the bed, my eyes scanning the room for any prying cameras. The thought of being watched is daunting, but my concern for Alicia overshadows it.

Yes, Nathan may catch me. But right now, that's a risk I have to take.

I pick up Alicia's tablet. My heart hammers against my ribcage, a symphony of fear and excitement. I open the device, my gaze flickering to the bathroom door every few seconds. The device hums in my hand, illuminating the room with its cold, harsh light.

The home screen reveals several open applications; a note-taking app lies obscured behind a digital paint program and a messaging platform. I navigate to her notes. A tap on the screen brings up the list of documents.

I see a list of documents, the dates going back months, all of them password-protected like the one I came across the other day—except for the one that's open right now. This one is unlocked. It appears to be a journal entry of some kind.

The medicine isn't working. Nathan keeps telling me it's just a matter of time before things improve, but it feels like I'm drowning. Every day is a battle against myself, against the confinement of this room, and I can't help wondering if he found out about the attorney.

Is he getting back at me? Is this his way of keeping me under control?

I try to think it all through, but the headaches obliterate my thoughts. Some days, all I can do is just lie in bed, praying for everything to stop moving—

I hear the jiggle of the bathroom door. Hastily returning the tablet to the place I found it, I retreat towards the window, pretending to adjust the curtains. My heart races in my chest, thudding so hard I fear Alicia might hear it. She walks back into the room, her gaze barely touching me before it returns to her tablet. I let out a breath I didn't realize I'd been holding, relief washing over me.

"Everything okay?" I ask, trying to keep my voice steady.

"It's fine," she says, her voice barely above a whisper as she retrieves her tablet and slips back into bed. And just like that, she retreats back into her world, leaving me alone with mine.

"Well," I say with a nervous smile, "let me know if you need anything."

She nods without looking up, and I make a hasty retreat. As I close the door behind me, I think about that journal entry.

Attorney. Was she planning to divorce Nathan? Had she learned about his flirting with Rebecca Chen and decided she was done with him?

I don't know the answer to these questions…but I sense that if I'm really going to do my job and protect Alicia, I'm going to have to find out.

Even if it means crossing Nathan Sterling himself.

CHAPTER TEN

At 3:57 on the following day, I step outside to find Grant waiting for me in the driveway, leaning against the hood of a gleaming black Audi. "Ms. Just," he says, a polite smile on his face. The golden sunlight washes his hair, and for a moment he seems less like an assistant for a tech mogul and more like something out of a Hollywood movie.

He is dressed in khaki shorts, a white button-down shirt that fits him perfectly, and sunglasses that only enhance his enigmatic aura. His eyes are hidden behind the dark lenses, but I can feel his gaze surveying me.

It's strange seeing anyone associated with the Sterlings dressed so informally. Perhaps it's a reminder that even though Grant works closely with Nathan, he's not really one of the Sterlings—a refreshing discovery.

For my part, I am dressed in a simple sundress, its sky-blue hue matching the perfect summer day around us. A pair of well-worn sandals adorns my feet and my carry bag hangs from one shoulder, stuffed with whatever I could find in a hurry: sunscreen, towel, phone, an old book I've been meaning to finish. I am wearing a bathing suit beneath the dress, too, but whether I will need it remains to be seen. As charming as Grant may be, I still hardly know the man.

"Mr. Davis," I say with equal formality. I can only remain serious for a few steps as I approach him, however—it all seems so silly, these unnecessary terms, and suddenly a smile breaks out across my face. The smile must be infectious because soon Grant is smiling as well, and then we both laugh like old college friends.

"You really are beautiful, Emily," Grant says, his laughter fading into an earnest look as he studies me as if for the first time. His sudden compliment catches me off guard, my laughter fizzling out as a blush creeps up my cheeks.

"Thank you, Grant," I stammer, painfully self-conscious beneath his gaze. "So this is your car?"

I gesture at the Audi in a desperate attempt to divert his focus.

"Yes," he replies, pushing off from the hood. "I got it from Nathan. It was one of his 'old' ones, if you can believe it. I don't think he ever drove it more than a handful of times before he was onto the next shiny thing."

I run my fingers along the cool, gleaming metal of the car, marveling at how far I am from my small-town Ohio beginnings. The realization is bittersweet as I recall the second-hand Buick my mother drove, always one breakdown away from the junkyard.

Grant's voice snaps me out of my thoughts. "Ready to go?"

"Sure," I say, trying to infuse some cheerfulness into my tone. The truth is I feel nervous—nervous about driving alone with this man I hardly know, nervous about spending the rest of the afternoon at the beach with him. Will he pick a secluded spot with nobody else in sight? What if something happens? We haven't even discussed when we'll return, so perhaps he intends to stay past dark.

It's all so open-ended, so full of possibilities, both thrilling and terrifying.

"Alright then," he says, opening the car door for me. I climb in, acutely aware of his gaze on me. Once we're both settled inside the luxurious vehicle, he revs up the engine and off we go.

I stare out the window, watching the Sterlings' domain recede. The Pacific is only a few minutes away, but I don't know how much longer it may take to park. What do I do with my hands, fold them in my lap? Let them rest on my legs?

"I'm glad to see you're feeling better," Grant says. "The way you ran from me yesterday..." He shakes his head, his eyebrows raised. "I thought you were in serious danger."

Heat rises to my face. "You must think I'm such a silly ninny," I mumble, picking at a loose thread on my sundress.

"Silly ninny?"

"It's a term my mother used to use."

"Very old-fashioned."

We're both silent for a few moments.

"You know," Grant says, "that's something I like about you—you're not desperate to keep up with the times, not rushing after the latest gadget like so many others of our generation."

Our generation. He must be close to thirty, given his statement that he was hired after graduating college seven years ago, while I am twenty-three. But perhaps it's not a significant distinction. The older you get, the less of a difference a few years makes.

“I suppose it’s an old habit,” I say, still gazing through the window. “We didn’t have much growing up, so I learned to make do without all the latest things.”

The scenes outside have changed from the wealthy neighborhood to an open road surrounded by large trees and fields. Then a glimpse of the majestic ocean emerges between the gaps in the pines, shrinking then expanding as we drive along the winding road.

There's an unsettling feeling gnawing at me: one part excitement amplified by the breathtaking view, two parts anxiety as I sit here with Grant—a man who is almost a stranger despite our sort-of friendship that has developed over the past week.

“Must be a bit of a shock, then,” he answers. “Living with the Sterlings, I mean.”

I make a sound that’s half-laugh, half-grunt. “You could say that.”

“It was a shock for me at first, too.”

“Yeah?” I ask, turning to face him, happy to be out of the spotlight.

He nods, flicking a brief glance my way before focusing back on the winding road. “Can you imagine? I was fresh out of college, hired by one of the world’s biggest tech moguls. It was like a dream come true.”

A sudden bout of curiosity takes over, and I ask, "What was it like? Your first time with them?"

Grant chuckles, running a hand through his hair. “Intimidating. Nathan has a way of filling up a room, you know? His presence is...it's just something else.” He turns to me, his eyes reflective. “And Alicia...she was so beautiful.”

My heart quickens at that. I've seen pictures of Alicia in her better days: vibrant, almost glowing with life. It's hard to reconcile that image with the woman upstairs, barely existing inside her gilded cage.

“She was a lot different then, too,” he continues. “She used to chat with the staff, hang out with Chloe, host lavish parties—all while helping Nathan keep the business afloat. She was a force to be reckoned with."

I try to imagine the woman he’s describing, but I can’t. The Alicia I know is timid and withdrawn, afraid of the outside world. She is the very opposite of a force to be reckoned with—now she is very little more than a nuisance to be put up with.

Then I pause, pondering something he said. "Alicia helped run the business?" I ask.

He glances at me, surprised by the question. "Oh…well…everyone had their part to play, right? Like I said, she did a lot of entertaining, so when it came to meeting with other leaders in the industry or investors, she was practically everywhere, filling glasses and clearing tables and popping into conversations to save Nathan from embarrassing himself when he bored guests with technical details." He chuckles, but the sound is strained.

"But she wasn't actually involved in the company?" I ask. "Wasn't part of the brain trust, so to speak?"

"Oh, heavens, no. She had no interest."

I nod, absorbing this. I still sense he's avoiding something, but I don't know how to get at it. Instead, I ask, "When did things go wrong? When did she start becoming afraid of the outside world, I mean?"

Grant's lips twitch as if he's contemplating how to answer. His eyebrows are lowered, his eyes cloudy as he studies the road. Finally, he shakes his head. "That's above my pay grade, I'm afraid," he says. "Besides, who can tell with things like this? It's like getting a cold: Sometimes you just wake up sick, and there's no telling where it came from."

I nod, but I'm unconvinced. Is he telling the truth? Or is he lying, perhaps to protect Nathan?

I pivot to a different question that's been on my mind. "I talked with Nathan and he made it sound like he's not the one who hired me."

Grant frowns. "What are you talking about? If he didn't hire you, then who? Alicia?"

"You?"

Grant snorts. "Me? Sure, Nathan and I work together, but his personal affairs are his personal affairs. If he didn't hire you, then I'm just as puzzled as you are."

Maybe Nathan simply forgot, or maybe he delegated the task of hiring an aide to someone else—Lena, for example. It doesn't matter.

Does it?

I'm distracted from these thoughts by the grinding of gravel beneath the tires as Grant pulls into a parking space near a small beachfront. The beach is deserted, save for a few seagulls picking at washed-up scraps. The waves crash into the shore rhythmically, creating a soothing white noise. A cool breeze carries with it salty spray and promises of relief from the anxious thoughts building in my mind.

"It's beautiful," I say, my gaze fixed on the vast expanse of the Pacific Ocean. I have never seen it before with my own eyes, not up close, and the sight is more awe-inspiring than I ever imagined. My chest expands with an indescribable feeling, both a fear of the unknown and a deeply rooted desire for freedom.

"Yeah, it is," Grant agrees. His voice is soft, almost reverent. He turns the car off, and several moments of silence pass between us, broken only by the lull of the ocean waves and the distant cries of seagulls.

"It's quiet here," I say, breaking the silence once more. "Peaceful."

"That's why I like it," he replies, his eyes never leaving the view in front of us. "It helps me think."

I wonder what he thinks about when he's here—the Sterlings' secrets? His own place in their elaborate, tech-laden world?

Or maybe he thinks about a girl. Is he dating anyone? The idea bothers me…but why? I hardly know him, and yet…

"You come here often?" I ask.

He looks at me then. There's a soft smile on his face, contrasting with a certain sadness in his gaze. "Whenever I get a chance," he replies, turning his gaze back to the horizon. "There's so much to think about, so much life to be lived. I won't always be Nathan's assistant, you know. I'm going to make a name for myself, leave my own mark on the world." He trails off, lost in thought.

Then he shakes himself suddenly and smiles. "Listen to me, rambling about my dreams when we've got the entire ocean right there in front of us."

Without waiting for a response, he pushes open the car door and steps out into the salty breeze. I watch him for a moment, his tall form silhouetted against the skyline, before deciding to push my own insecurities aside and following after him.

As my feet touch the sand, I feel a strange sensation of freedom. Back at the mansion, I'm always aware of eyes on me: security cameras, Alicia's fearful gaze, Grant's strange attentiveness, Lena's unrelenting scorn. But here there's no judgment, no pretense, just the endless ocean and the whispering wind.

Grant is standing near the water's edge when I catch up with him. The waves lap at his ankles as he looks out into the distance, his face thoughtful.

I step up beside him, my sandals sinking slightly into the wet sand. We stand in silence for a moment, both lost in our own thoughts. The rushing sound of the surf and the distant crying of seagulls are the only sounds that break the stillness.

"Why did you invite me out here?" I finally ask, emboldened by the silence. "You hardly know me."

He smiles, but it's a different kind of smile this time. It's more wistful, perhaps even melancholic. "That's precisely why I invited you out here." His voice is soft, nearly drowned out by the crashing waves. "In the mansion, everyone wears masks. Even you, Emily."

His words catch me off guard. What mask does he think I've been wearing? I have always felt like others can see right through me, so I'm puzzled by his words.

"You're not like the others," he continues. "You don't belong in that world of pretense. I thought...maybe you needed a break from it all, even if you didn't realize it yet."

He's right. The tension and anxiety have been building up inside me since the moment I stepped into that mansion. But now, on this desolate beach with the vast, beautiful ocean stretching out in front of us, I finally feel like I can breathe again.

"Thank you," I say, my gaze dropping to where the waves are lapping against his feet. I feel strangely drawn to him—not like a lover, exactly, but like he's my guardian. Rich would say I am looking for the father I never had, even in a man not much older than I am. Is that all this is? My desperation for someone to stand up for me, to pick me out of a crowd and show me I'm special to them?

I must have unconsciously leaned toward Grant, because suddenly I become aware of how close he and I are—the distance between us no more than a whisper. I wonder what it would feel like to press my body against his, feel his strength and vitality.

He turns toward me, staring down into my eyes. Neither of us is wearing a mask now, it seems, because the longing I see in his eyes is naked and hungry. His arm curls behind me, fingertips brushing my shoulder-blades, but just before his fingers can find their hold something buzzes against my arm.

It's my phone, vibrating inside my carry bag.

"Leave it," Grant says, taking my chin and turning my face back to his. But it's buzzing against me like an angry bee, too distracting to be ignored.

"One second," I say, pulling away.

Breathless, I retreat several paces before lowering the bag to the ground. As I do so, the mouth of the bag opens, and I see the screen of my phone lit up with a call from a number I don't know. I am about to leave it and turn back toward Grant when a text message appears.

Brimming with curiosity, I slid my thumb over the button so I can preview the message. The words rob me of what little breath I've managed to recover.

please call me as soon as you can. your life is in DANGER.

"Something wrong?" Grant asks.

Startled, I flip the phone face-down and rise, trying to smile. "Nothing at all," I say. "Just a call from a friend back in Ohio."

"A friend?" He arches an eyebrow as he approaches.

"Sadie," I say without thinking, then wince inwardly at the lie. "We haven't had a chance to connect since I left."

Why do I feel this need to lie to him? Does it say more about him or about me?

Grant nods. "Well, I'm sure you two can catch up later. It's not every day you get to stand on the shore of the world's largest ocean."

He is getting closer now, and part of me wants to let him put his arm around me and hold me close—and whatever else such intimacy might lead to. But I can't get that text out of my mind, and I won't be able to relax until I know what's going on.

"Actually," I say, "I think we should head back to the house. I'd like to talk with Sadie, and I'm sure she'll want a video tour."

Grant stares blankly at me for a few seconds, and I wonder if I've offended him. Then he nods, the gesture polite if not warm. "Of course. My wish is your command."

An awkward silence, thick as spider silk, stretches between us as we return to the vehicle. It remains there during the drive back to the house, but I am hardly aware of it.

I can't stop thinking about the words of the text—and wondering who sent them.

CHAPTER ELEVEN

"My name is Trevor Hammond," the voicemail says. "I worked for the company for five years, long enough to get a good read on them. And you need to understand just what they're capable of."

I am sitting in my bedroom, staring out the window as sunset bleeds over the rose garden. Inside the house, I can hear the faint hum of electronic devices, the distant footsteps of someone—Lena, probably—moving about. I already miss the ocean.

"We need to talk," the message continues. "As long as you're in that house, your life is in danger. You have no idea what you've gotten yourself into."

A chill runs down my spine as his words pour into my ear. There's an energy to Trevor's message, a desperation that causes my breath to hitch in my throat. Could this be a man scorned by Nathan, desperate for revenge? Or someone genuinely concerned about my welfare?

After fortifying myself with a few steady breaths, I get ready to call him back. But no—I can't call him here, where every word could be picked up. Maybe the bathroom? Surely the bathrooms aren't bugged. I'm pretty sure that would be illegal.

In the end, I opt to text him instead. Safer that way.

How do you know who I am? I write.

I set the phone aside, not really expecting a swift reply. But within a few moments, I receive an answering message.

Lets meet up—ill tell you everything. howards cafe, tomorrow at ten.

I lean back, unsure what to think. Am I really going to meet up with a man I know nothing about just because he claims to have valuable information? Even if I want to do so, the logistics are tricky. I'll have to find Howard's Cafe, a place I've never visited, and get a ride there as well. Not to mention explaining my absence to the ever-suspicious Lena.

But then...the possibility of danger. The risk of staying ignorant, of letting whatever trap Trevor thinks I've walked into snap shut around me. Is that a risk I'm willing to take?

I look down at my phone again, at Trevor's message. Someone is trying to help me here. Despite the alarm bells ringing in my head, despite the gnawing fear in my gut, there's also a spark of gratitude.

I grab my phone and quickly type out a response: *I'll be there.*

After I hit send, I sit back on my bed, staring blankly at the gaudy chandelier glinting from the ceiling. My heartbeat drums in my ears, drowning out the distant hum of the mansion's intricate machinery.

Restlessness gnaws at me, and I can't stay in my room any longer. I slip on a light jacket, deciding that a walk might do me some good. With my phone clutched nervously in hand, I head towards the grand staircase. Halfway down it, a voice calls out, "Ah, Emily. There you are."

I turn to see Lena moving toward me, a tight smile—all politeness, no warmth—stretching her lips back without revealing her teeth. My heart sinks. Whatever this is, it won't be good.

"I think there may be a bit of a misunderstanding as to your duties here," she adds.

"Misunderstanding?" I'm puzzled. Where is this going?

"I have been waiting on Alicia hand and foot today while you were off doing God-knows-what with Mr. Davis. Really, Emily, a little professionalism goes a long way."

My face colors at this. Alicia reassured me it would be fine if I left for a few hours, and I was gone far less than that. Suddenly, it all makes sense: Lena is getting back at me for catching her spying on Alicia's therapy session. Lena can't confront me directly—if she does that, I can reveal her spying—but she *can* make my life miserable.

I am so stunned by Lena's words that for a few moments, I can hardly speak. Anger, confusion, and embarrassment all bubble up at once.

"I'll overlook it this time," Lena says, inspecting a lampshade for dust. "But if you should neglect your duties again, I will have no choice but to inform Mr. Sterling. Given the degree of latitude he's granted you to perform your duties, I think he would be very disappointed to hear how you took advantage of his lenience today."

Now the anger pushes itself to the forefront. She is so condescending, so cruel. Is this her way of making herself feel better? She is a servant herself, not a social equal with the Sterlings, but perhaps if she puts me down, she can feel better about her own station.

Lena's eyes dart toward me, studying me. I sense she is waiting for me to lash out...and for that very reason, I decide not to give her the satisfaction.

“I will go check on Mrs. Sterling right now,” I say.

And with that, I turn and continue down the staircase, leaving Lena behind me without another word. I can almost feel her eyes burning into my back as I descend the last steps.

As soon as I'm out of sight, I begin to tremble. Lena's words echo in my head. I hate the control that bitter, humorless woman exerts over me. Everything is a chess match with her, a zero-sum game where my loss is her gain.

I make my way to Alicia’s suite, hoping she won’t sense my anxiety. Knocking lightly on the heavy oak door, I push it open when I hear a murmured "come in."

Alicia is huddled on her bed, her pale skin almost translucent against the dark duvet. Her listless eyes turn towards me, glinting with a hint of relief.

"Emily," she whispers, managing a frail smile. "You're here."

"Of course," I reply, forcing a calmness into my voice that I don’t feel. I stride over and sit beside her on the bed. "Is something wrong?"

To my surprise, Alicia’s fingers reach out to brush against mine. She has never touched me before, has never shown this degree of vulnerability.

Did something happen while I was gone?

“Lena has been fluttering around me like a bird all afternoon,” she says. “I would fire that woman if I didn’t know Nathan would just overrule my decision.”

I frown, wondering what to make of this. “What do you have against Lena?”

Alicia sighs heavily, sinking back into her pillows. "It's not that I have anything against her specifically. It's just...she smothers me. Always hovering, always watching. And I can't stand it. It makes the walls of this house feel even smaller."

I nod, understanding. "I could speak with her, if you'd like…" I trail off, quickly realizing it’s an ill-conceived idea.

Alicia looks at me for a moment, and I see something pass over her eyes—fear? caution?—before she shakes her head. "No, that's not necessary. I'd prefer if you didn't get involved. you’ll only upset her."

I have no doubt she’s right.

Alicia gazes at the ceiling, chewing her lip like a lonely child. “There is so much I would say if I could just…find the right words.” She glances at me, and there’s something lively in her glance—something that communicates there’s more to her words than the words themselves.

What is she trying to say?

"I'm happy to listen," I say.

She shakes her head. "My mind is all confused—it would just make things worse. I shouldn't talk until I can be clearer." Again, she gives me that look. What is she trying to convey? Is she saying we need to find somewhere private to talk, away from cameras and microphones?

Or am I imagining this subtext to her speech?

With a quick breath, she pushes the sheets back and rises, heading for the bathroom. Inventing a pretext on the spot, I hurry toward her. "Here, let me help you," I say as I take her arm. "You seem a little unsteady."

She makes no comment, and I help her into the bathroom. As the door closes, I glance around.

No cameras in here, at least not that I can see.

I turn to Alicia and put my hands on her shoulders. She seems surprised, but she studies my eyes, waiting.

"I know something's going on," I say in a low voice. "I know you're a prisoner here."

She bites her lip and says nothing. Knowing it will be suspicious if I stay long, I decide to try another tact.

"Do you know someone named Trevor Hammond?" I ask.

Recognition flashes across Alicia's face—recognition and fear.

"I…I've never heard that name," she says, shaking her head. But her face says otherwise.

"It's okay. It's just me. You can be honest."

"I'm sorry, I don't know this person." She jabs a finger at the wall, and I reluctantly follow her pointing finger. There, hidden unobtrusively in the wall, designed to blend in seamlessly with its surroundings, is a speaker. A microphone.

Which means that if Nathan is listening in, I have just shown him my hand.

CHAPTER TWELVE

I knock on Chloe's door and wait, shifting impatiently from one foot to the other.

No answer. It's six o'clock, so I know she hasn't left for school yet. She's probably still sleeping. I can only imagine how annoyed she'll be at me for waking her, but this is too important to worry about her feelings.

After my last encounter with Lena and her insinuation that I was 'neglecting my duties,' I am very nervous about stealing away from the property to meet with Trevor Hammond at Howard's Cafe in four hours. If she reports me to Nathan—and I feel certain she will if I give her any more ammunition—Nathan may fire me, and I will not only lose a well-paying job that can help me earn my master's degree.

I will also lose the chance to help Alicia from this conspiracy of control.

If anyone can help me avoid detection, it's Chloe.

I knock again, louder this time, and after a moment the door swings open. Chloe squints at me from the threshold, her hair in wild disarray and her eyes puffy with sleep.

"What do you want?" she grumbles.

"I thought we could talk," I say, trying not to reveal my intentions to anyone who may be listening in. She raises an eyebrow but shrugs and steps aside to let me in.

Her bed is disheveled, and clothes are scattered haphazardly around the room. She plops back down onto her mattress, pulling a pillow over her face. "What's really going on?" she mumbles into the fabric.

Before launching into my explanation, I turn on a nearby fan to the highest setting. It doesn't make a great deal of noise, so I open my phone. "You ever listen to punk rock?" I ask.

"Sure…" she says, sounding both baffled and a bit annoyed.

I turn on a punk rock station and raise the volume. It's loud, but even so, I make sure to get close to Chloe and lower my voice, hoping no hidden microphones will pick up my words.

"I need to get off the property for a little while without anyone noticing...especially Lena."

Chloe sits up, clearly intrigued. “Thus the loud music—makes sense. Who’s the lucky fellow?”

I shake my head. “It’s not like that. This is…more serious.”

I expect her to ask more questions, perhaps to make a few jokes at my expense, but instead she merely raises an eyebrow. "I’m listening," she says, the sleepiness finally gone from her eyes.

“There’s not much more.” I hesitate, then decide to press on. I have no choice but to trust her. “Someone who claims he used to work for your father sent me a message. He told me my life is in danger.”

Chloe frowns. "What's his name?"

"Trevor Hammond."

Chloe's face remains blank, revealing no reaction.

“I need to go speak with him face-to-face,” I add. “At ten this morning. But Lena’s been on my case lately, and if she realizes I’m gone…well, she’ll definitely tell your father. I might lose my job.”

A hint of a smile appears on Chloe’s face. It would seem that the prospect of mischief has finally captured her interest. She swings her legs around, hopping out of bed and hurriedly pulling on a crumpled hoodie from the floor. I watch her, surprised by this sudden burst of energy.

“What’s…going on?” I ask. “I know you have to get ready for school—”

"Not anymore," she says. "School's canceled today, didn't you hear?" She gives me an impish smile. "And you can turn off that music—I already clawed apart all the cameras and speakers installed in here."

I have to say, I’m impressed by her audacity. I turn off the music.

“I wasn’t asking you to play hooky,” I say.

“What’s hooky?”

“It’s when you—never mind. The point is, it’s only gonna make things worse if you miss school because of me.”

Chloe shrugs. “I miss school all the time anyway—one more day won't make a difference. Besides," she grins mischievously, "I've got a plan."

I raise an eyebrow, intrigued despite myself. "A plan?"

"Yeah," Chloe says, holding up a finger and heading towards her en-suite bathroom. Amid the sound of running water, I hear her continue. "First, we need to get you out of the house without Lena seeing. That part's easy—I'll distract her."

The prospect of Chloe going toe-to-toe with Lena worries me. "You sure you want to take that on?"

Her laughter echoes from the bathroom. "Lena? No problem. I've been dealing with her since diapers, Emily. Trust me."

I nod, but my anxiety is far from assuaged. Still, she knows Lena much better than I do.

Chloe emerges moments later, her hair tamed into a messy bun atop her head, her face scrubbed clean of any lingering sleepiness. She's all bright eyes and energy now, like a different person from the sullen teenager who answered my knocking moments before.

"Second," she continues, as if there's been no interruption, "we need to make sure no one notices you're gone. But that's easy enough."

"How's that?"

She shrugs. "You tell Lena I wasn't feeling well and I demanded you wait on me, hand and foot."

I arch an eyebrow. "My job is to take care of your mother, not you."

"That's true. But you can just say Mom dismissed you—she does it anyway, doesn't she?"

I wish I could argue, but it's true that Alicia has no use for me most of the time.

Chloe grins at me, triumphant. "Just do as I say, and trust me. We'll get you out of here."

I can't fully ignore the fluttering anxiety in my chest, but there's something about Chloe's confidence, her impulsiveness even, that brings a gust of fresh air into the stale mansion. Plus, I really have no choice.

With a resigned sigh, I nod. "Fine. But even if this distraction of yours works, how do I get outside without being noticed? Every door and window in this place is monitored."

Her eyes flash with delight.

"You sneak out," I say, shaking my head admiringly.

She shrugs one shoulder while inspecting her fingernails. "From time to time. I've discovered that if you go out my bathroom window and down the ivy trellis, the cameras don't catch you. A blind spot, I guess."

"I'm not exactly an expert climber," I say dubiously.

"It's not that hard, promise," she reassures me, her eyes sparkling with mischief. "Besides, we're not exactly spoiled for options here, are we?"

"No," I admit reluctantly.

"Now that we're agreed, go on downstairs and tell Lena I'm not feeling well."

I move toward the door, then pause and look back at her. "Why are you helping me?"

Chloe looks at me for a moment, her blue eyes filled with a defiance that seems both precocious and vulnerable. "Because you don't look at me like I'm some project that needs fixing."

Her words stun me into silence.

This young girl, who had at first seemed so aloof and rebellious, suddenly lays bare an understanding beyond her sixteen years. I offer a small smile of gratitude, touched by her honesty and the strange camaraderie forming between us, two outsiders in the Sterling mansion.

Moving swiftly down the grand staircase, I make my way to Lena in the kitchen. Anxiety twists my stomach into knots. This is a dangerous game we're playing—it might seem silly to Chloe, but for me, I could lose my job if Lena discovers the truth.

"Morning, Lena," I say, attempting to keep my voice steady and casual.

The housekeeper glances up from where she's chopping vegetables for lunch, a look of surprise on her face. "Emily? What are you doing down here so early?"

"Chloe isn't feeling well," I lie smoothly, praying that my face doesn't betray the fiction I am spinning. "She asked me to stay with her."

Lena narrows her eyes, her wrinkles deepening with suspicion. "That girl is as fit as a fiddle. Are you sure she didn't just trick you into getting her out of studying?"

I do my best to look hurt. "She really seemed unwell, Lena. I think it's best I keep an eye on her. I came down to see if there's any soup I can take her."

Lena studies me for a moment, her gaze sharp and penetrating, before she finally relents. "There's some chicken soup in the fridge you can heat up for her."

"Thank you," I say, hoping she can't hear my relief.

As I open the fridge and search for the soup, Lena says, "Don't forget your job is to take care of Alicia, not Chloe. She still needs her pills at nine o'clock sharp. I can look after Chloe myself." Even as she says the words, however, I sense a note of false bravado. I get the distinct impression Lena would rather keep her distance from Chloe. She's probably relieved that I've volunteered to take care of the girl myself.

I can only imagine the pranks Chloe has played on the housekeeper over the years.

I give Lena a small smile. "Of course—I'll make sure Alicia gets her medication on schedule. I just thought I'd save you some trouble while she rests."

Ignoring the unsure expression on her face, I place the soup in a bowl and heat it up, then cover it with a lid so as not to spill any during my return trip. "Thanks again," I say over my shoulder as I leave the kitchen. I wait for her to call me back, to tell me she doesn't believe me, but neither happens.

I continue upstairs, back to Chloe. She's lounging on her bed when I enter, engrossed in her phone. Her eyes flick up at me and I nod, indicating that our plan is in motion.

"Here's your soup," I say, putting it down on her bedside table. "I hope you feel better soon."

She rolls her eyes. "When did you say your not-a-date is?"

"Ten o'clock."

She puffs her lips out in a tired breath. "We've got a few hours to kill, then."

"I still have to give your mother her pills, but yes, otherwise we've got time." I pause, studying the mischievous glint in her cerulean eyes. "I get the impression you have some ideas."

"We could snoop around my dad's study," she suggests.

I jolt at her suggestion. "That's not a good idea."

She shrugs nonchalantly. "He's at a meeting all day, and Grant is out running errands for him. No one will know."

"But what if we get caught?"

She just rolls her eyes at me. "Scaredy-cat," she says. "If you're not up for that, then I guess we'll have to resort to the old reliable." She leans down and pulls a worn, torn board game from beneath the bed.

Monopoly.

The idea of the two of us playing Monopoly together is so mundane, so utterly *normal*, that it almost jars me.

"What?" she asks, frowning. "Don't tell me you've never played."

"No, of course I've played. It's just, the last time I played…" I trail off, troubled by a memory. "It's a long story."

"Then it's perfect," she says as she opens the box. "We've got plenty of time."

I don't usually talk about that part of my life, but she's so earnest and innocent—not to mention the fact that she's going out of her way to help me. How can I not be open with her?

"The last time I played this game was with Sadie," I said.

“Who’s Sadie?” She is now pulling the pieces from the box, setting up the board on the bed between us.

“My best friend. Or she was.” I shrug, trying to keep my voice steady.

“Was?”

“She died in high school. Car accident.”

Chloe’s playful demeanor instantly vanishes. “I’m sorry, Emily. I didn’t know.”

“It’s okay. You remind me of her, actually. She was always up for mischief, never afraid of anything. Being around her…it was like anything could happen.” A small smile forms on my lips at the memory.

“I think I’d like her.”

“I think you would.”

We both fall silent for a few moments. Chloe begins dealing with money, but her movements are slow and contemplative.

“This accident,” she says. “Were you in the vehicle?”

I nod slowly, taking a deep breath to steady myself before I answer. It's been years, but the memory is still just as visceral. "Yeah, I was."

She gives a small nod of understanding and doesn't probe any further. There's something very mature about her in these few moments, and it makes me think that maybe Chloe Sterling isn't as bratty as I thought when I first met her.

To my surprise, I find myself volunteering more. “My boyfriend, Dillon, was driving at the time. We’d just come from a party, and I could tell Dillon had had too much to drink. But he kept saying he was fine and I was too afraid to confront him, to insist that he shouldn't drive."

I pause, swallowing past the lump in my throat. "He swerved off the road and hit a tree. He was fine, barely had a scratch, and I didn’t get anything worse than a few bruises. But Sadie…Sadie wasn’t so lucky.”

Chloe is silent for a while, her eyes downcast. "I'm sorry," she says again, softly this time, and I know she means it.

"For the longest time I kept imagining I could go back," I murmur almost to myself. "I saw myself pulling the keys out of Dillon’s hand and just flinging them into the darkness. He gets angry at me, starts yelling, but I don’t care because I know Sadie is going to be alright. I know that in an hour or two, she’s going to be safe in her own bed, sound asleep.”

I sigh and shake my head. “But that’s just living in denial, isn’t it? Refusing to believe it really happened and there’s nothing I can do to change it?”

There’s something else underneath the denial, too, a buried anger at having been abandoned by Sadie just as I was abandoned by my father. Sadie may not have wanted to leave me, and in that sense the two are very different, but the harsh reality is that they’re both gone.

“Everyone leaves,” I mutter with a bitter smile. “Story of my life.”

“I know how that feels.”

I frown at her. I don’t want to come across as condescending, but how can she know how it feels?

“I feel like I lost my mom a while ago,” she continues, her voice dropping to a near whisper. "She may still be here physically, but she's not really here anymore. And my dad's always so caught up in his work. He cares, he really does, but sometimes it feels like he's more of a boss than a father."

Chloe's eyes are distant as she speaks, as if seeing something I can't. A loneliness that perhaps I understand more than I'd like to admit.

"I'm sorry," I say. "That must be really hard."

"Yeah," she nods slowly. "It is. It happened so gradually, you know? First, Mom stopped going out—she'd complain about headaches or just being tired. And I'm sure she *was* tired—she hardly ever slept through the night. She'd get up and walk around, just wander aimlessly. One time I caught her having a full-blown conversation with herself about whether plants can feel pain."

Chloe shakes her head sadly. "Next thing I know, she's sleeping more and more and Dad has this expert brought in, some guy Grant found."

"Dr. Harris."

"Yeah. And once she started taking those pills..." Chloe swallowed hard. "It might have leveled her out, but now I almost don't recognize her at all."

It's strange—I'd assumed Nathan hired Dr. Harris, but more and more it seems like he just rubber-stamped Grant's decision. It reminds me of Lena's remark about it being 'Grant's orders' not to take any books from the library.

Who is actually in charge here?

"Sometimes it's hard to remember what she was like," Chloe says pensively. "Back before all this started."

That reminds me of a question that's been on my mind. "Chloe…back when your father started AltoTech, was your mother involved?"

"Of course," Chloe replies immediately.

"More than entertaining and that kind of thing, I mean. Involved in the design of the technology."

"Yes. She practically founded the company herself—it never would've happened without her ideas, her algorithms. She might not look it, but she's every bit as brilliant as my dad—and much more organized. She still found time to be a mother, though. Somehow."

Why, I wonder, did Grant tell me Alicia wasn't involved? It's hard to chalk that up to forgetfulness…but the only alternative is to conclude he lied to me.

Why would he want to keep Alicia's involvement in the company a secret?

A heavy silence settles between us and for the first time since I arrived at the Sterling mansion, I sense a genuine connection with Chloe. A shared understanding of what it feels like to be left, to be forgotten.

Suddenly, the mansion doesn't seem so cold, so foreign. Perhaps it's not the place itself but the people within it that make it seem intimidating.

"Chloe," I say carefully. "I'm going to do everything I can to help your mother get well again. Whatever it takes, understand?"

Chloe nods, regarding me curiously as if searching for a message hidden in my words.

"If I need your help to do that," I continue, "can I count on it?"

She studies the game board and says nothing for several long seconds. Then she looks me square in the eye, her jaw set and her nostrils flaring. "If you can show my mother how to be a mother again…there's nothing in the world I won't do to help."

CHAPTER THIRTEEN

The time has come. With Chloe's help, I climb up into the bathroom window, then turn around and prepare to lower myself down the ivy trellis.

It's 9:40 in the morning, and there is an Uber waiting for me down the street to take me to Howard's Cafe, where I will meet with the mysterious Trevor Hammond at 10. I am not sure what he will have to say, other than some explanation as to why he warned me that my life is in danger, but I am hopeful that he may provide some insights into the Sterling family.

And specifically into the mysterious development of Alicia’s condition.

"Remember," Chloe says, "you're just going out for a quick coffee. You'll be back before anyone even realizes you're gone."

I nod, holding onto her encouraging gaze as I begin my descent. The brick wall is rough under my fingers, the ivy's leaves soft as they glide against my skin. My heart beats wildly in my chest as the ground comes closer and closer. My sneakers land softly on the manicured lawn, barely making a noise.

I straighten up, take one last glance at Chloe who's watching anxiously from above, and then quickly move along the side of the mansion, blending into the shadows as best as I can.

I pause at the corner, recalling Chloe's instructions as best I can. According to her, if I can get around to the far side of the rose garden, the wall of blooms will shield me from the house's view and allow me to slip over the hill at the edge of the property. From there I can make my way down the driveway, staying hidden behind the hill until I reach the place where my Uber is parked.

I sure hope nobody notices the parked car before I get there and grows suspicious.

I blow out a breath, swallow my anxiety, and take my first step onto the cobblestone pathway. The promise of uncovering the truth about Alicia and the Sterlings drags me forward. I stick to the path, careful to avoid the security cameras that Chloe has warned me about, tucked away in the canopy of trees and among the stone sculptures that litter the expansive garden.

The rose garden is just ahead, its vibrant colors muted by a low-lying fog. I glance over my shoulder once more, making sure no one's following me, then duck behind a large marble statue of Aphrodite, hiding in her shadow until I'm sure it's safe to continue.

I'm going to feel so silly if I run into Grant.

A hushed sigh escapes my lips as I creep along the side of the towering rosebushes, their thorns scratching at my arms and legs through my clothes. The perfume of the roses is overwhelming but somehow comforting, a reminder that beneath all the cold technology and surveillance there's still something natural, something alive in this place.

Finally, I reach the garden's edge and the hill Chloe had mentioned. I glance back towards the mansion one last time, half-expecting to see someone racing towards me. But everything is quiet. Maybe Chloe was right; maybe they really wouldn't notice I was gone.

I duck low and scramble up the hill, keeping my body pressed close to the ground. The grass feels cool and dewy under my palms, the misty morning air wrapping around me like a shroud. I'm hidden from sight now, the Sterling mansion concealed behind the veil of fog and flora.

The driveway is just ahead of me, a stretch of sleek gray concrete lined with tall trees to either side. I glance around quickly before making a run for it, my heart pounding in sync with each step.

The Uber appears as a vague silhouette in the distance, its headlights cutting through the thick curtain of fog. I break into a run, slipping past the last stretch of trees and out onto the open road. The car's back door swings open, revealing a darkened interior. I glance back once more for good measure, but there's only silence behind me. I've made it.

I slide into the backseat of the car, chest heaving from both exertion and adrenaline as I buckle myself in. The driver, a middle-aged man with graying hair and kind eyes, barely glances at me in the rearview mirror before he pulls away from the curb.

I can only imagine what he thinks of the strange set of instructions I gave him when I paid him to pick me up. Good thing I'm giving him a generous tip taken from my first week's earnings.

If the driver is at all curious about my need for secrecy, he says nothing about it. It's just as well. I need a few moments to gather my thoughts before meeting this Trevor Hammond. I have to be on my A-game, have to keep my wits about me. I can't trust him simply because he claims to be looking out for me.

The drive into town is quick, but it feels endless. The fog outside has now turned into a heavy rain, transforming the world into a blurry watercolor painting.

The Uber pulls up to a small, vintage cafe across from the post office. The cafe looks like it's stuck in the sixties, not through neglect but rather an intentional focus on the past. The beaten red-brick exterior, the soft yellow glow from the window, and the sound of Ella Fitzgerald's voice floating through the air in dulcet tones create a scene straight out of a time capsule.

I step out of the Uber, thanking the driver with a shaky smile before he speeds off into the rain. I paid him on the app, so there's no need to exchange cash.

My pulse quickens as I approach the cafe's door, my hand hovering over the handle. It's a brave new world on the other side, filled with unknown secrets and dangerous revelations.

Swallowing my fear, I push open the door and step inside. The café is cozy and surprisingly warm despite its retro aesthetic. Vintage posters line the walls, and a jukebox in the corner starts up an old Sinatra tune as Fitzgerald's song ends. A handful of patrons sit scattered at various tables, some hunched over their coffee cups, others engaged in hushed conversation. The sharp scent of espresso and the faint undercurrent of cinnamon and baked goods fill the air, soothing my heightened nerves.

I scan the room, heart pounding as I search for Trevor, although I have no real idea what he looks like. Why didn't I Google him before coming here? Rookie mistake.

Then again…it's not like I'm a trained detective. I don't do this sort of thing—clandestine meetings at cafes. I will just have to find a seat and hope Trevor finds me. He found my name with no trouble, so he's probably already figured out what I look like.

Anxiety claws its way up my throat as I make my way to the counter to order a coffee, my eyes darting over the display case full of pastries. I haven't eaten anything this morning, but I'm not about to try now. My stomach is far too unsettled for that.

"Can I help you?" the barista asks, her bright smile jarring me out of my thoughts. She's young, younger than me, with a nose piercing and short pink hair that somehow fits perfectly within the vintage aesthetic of the café.

"Yes," I mutter, glancing briefly at the board. "A medium coffee, please."

As she prepares my coffee, I scan the room again. There's a man in a suit sitting by himself near the back, scrolling through his phone with an air of impatience. Could he be Trevor? Or maybe it's the guy in the corner booth with a baseball cap pulled low over his eyes, his face obscured by the morning paper.

The barista hands me my coffee and I pay, my hands trembling just enough to spill a few drops onto the counter. I apologize, but she just smiles and wipes it up.

"First time here?" she asks, her eyes warm and sympathetic.

I nod, giving her a tight smile before turning away. Time to find a seat.

I choose a small table near the center of the cafe, close enough to the counter to keep an eye on the door, but far enough away to not draw attention. I pull out the chair, the scraping sound loud in my ears against the background of quiet chatter and clinking dishes. I sit down stiffly, maintaining an upright posture that probably screams discomfort.

Taking small sips from my piping hot coffee to calm my frazzled nerves, I keep glancing at the cafe entrance. Every chime of the door sends a jolt of anticipation through me, but if Trevor has walked in, he doesn't seem to have noticed me.

Without warning, a voice behind me causes me to jump, nearly spilling coffee all over my blouse.

"Sorry for the cloak-and-dagger," the voice says.

I turn and see none other than Marcus Welby standing at my table, his chest puffed out, his hands in his pockets.

Shocked, I start to rise. "Marcus, what are you—"

"No need to get up." He smiles, but there's a note of tension in his voice. "Thought I'd introduce you and Mr. Hammond. I am, after all, the one who gave him your number."

Well, that explains one little mystery.

"He's a very cautious man after what happened," Marcus says. "So whatever you do, don't make a scene."

"Is he here now?"

Marcus drifts away without another word. I sit down again, feeling like I'm in a spy movie. It's both thrilling and frightening at the same time.

“This seat taken?” A man stands at my elbow, gesturing at the chair beside me.

"No," I say. "Go ahead."

He drags the chair to the table behind me. Then I hear him sit down. A few moments later, I hear him murmur, "Don't turn around. Pull out your phone and pretend you're scrolling."

My heart skips a beat. Trevor Hammond—it has to be. His voice is low and firm and utterly serious. I fumble to pull out my phone, my hand trembling lightly against the cold plastic.

Swallowing back the wave of trepidation gripping me, I unlock my device and pretend to scroll through a sea of messages and notifications. I turn my head and, out of the corner of my eye, I steal a glance at the man beside me. He is wearing faded, washed-out jeans and a nondescript gray hoodie. He has a breakfast sandwich on the table in front of him, along with a tablet displaying a spreadsheet.

"I said don't turn around," he says, his voice stern but no louder than before.

"Is this really necessary?" I ask as I turn my attention back to my phone.

"If you knew who you were living with, you'd understand. From this point on, no names—I know who you are, you know who I am."

Trevor's warning causes me to shudder. I take a gulp of my coffee, trying to ignore the tremble in my hand.

"Okay," I say. "So…what did you want to talk about?"

He's silent for a moment. "Why did you become a home aide?"

The question surprises me, and I pause for a moment. "To save up money." I hardly know this man—I have no obligation to share every last detail with him, not when he hasn't earned my trust.

"Is that it?" he asks. "Just for the money?"

"Well, no. I like helping people, too."

"Helping, or saving?"

I start to twist around. "What are you getting at?"

"Eyes forward." There's a hint of something else in his voice now. Fear.

I untwist and stare at the drops racing down the window.

"He's watching you now," Trevor continues in a lower voice. "Anyone in that house is under his thumb. You have no idea the lives he's destroyed—and I mean lives, not just careers. He loves one thing: power. That's his god."

"You said you worked there—" I almost said 'at AltoTech,' but stopped myself—"for five years?"

"That's right."

"And then you quit? Because of how he was treating you?"

Trevor laughs, but there's no humor in the sound. "Quit? I was forced out. The truth is, I had discovered some…less than savory business practices. Back doors in government security software, the kind you could sell to hackers for quite a profit."

"And you confronted him about it?"

"I did. He claimed he knew nothing about it and said he'd look into it. Next thing I know, I'm being accused of embezzlement—and I can hardly defend myself, because the proof is right there on my workstation. He even deposited money into my savings account to sell the lie."

His words fall heavily between us. I say nothing, aware that my heart is pounding in my chest.

"So why are you warning me now?" I ask after a beat. "Why help me?"

"Because I don't want them to do to you what they did to me." He drops his voice even further. "I'm working on building a case against him…but it's taking time. The best thing you can do is make an excuse to get out of there and never look back."

"You have proof about those backdoors?"

"Oh, I know something even more damning than that."

I sit in silence for a few moments, absorbing this. Is he right? Did I make a mistake getting involved in the Sterlings' lives? Maybe the best thing would be to get a job somewhere less complicated, less dangerous, where I can just keep my head down and do the work and not have to worry about being watched and controlled.

As I imagine quitting, though, I see Alicia's face loom before me: innocent, child-like, pleading. I hear the echo of the promise I made to Chloe just a few hours ago: *I'm going to do everything I can to help your mother get healthy again.*

"I could help you, you know," I finally say. "We could work together to bring him down."

Trevor sighs. "As tempting as the offer is, I can't ask you to risk your life over this—I don't need that on my conscience. Nor can I risk him getting wind of my plans. No, your part in this is over."

I shake my head. "I have to help her. It might be dangerous, but it's what I have to do. I'm not leaving."

There's a long silence. A Rolling Stones tune starts up on the jukebox.

"You're making a mistake," he says heavily. "You can't save her, no matter how hard you try."

"Why's that?"

He pushes back his chair and stands. "Because it's already too late for her—and if you don't get out while you can, it'll be too late for you, too."

CHAPTER FOURTEEN

Chloe's hand reaches down as I near the window, and she helps me off the trellis and into her bathroom again.

"So?" she asks, studying me with a curious frown. "Is your life really in danger, or was it just a new pick-up tactic?"

I brush a few leaves off my blouse. "I don't know what to think," I murmur. "He didn't give me much new information."

I'm unsure how much to share with her. Should I tell her that an ex-employee of her father's is building a case to destroy her father and everything he's worked for? Chloe is clearly not close with her father, but that doesn't mean she wants to see his life ruined. And telling her these details could complicate her willingness to help me in the future.

She's watching me, one hand cocked on her hip. "Come on," she says. "I skipped school for you, and now I've gotta pretend to be sick the rest of the day. You need to do better than 'I don't know what to think.'"

I sigh. "Alright," I say, deciding to share a watered-down version of Trevor's ominous warnings. "He says that your father has a lot of enemies—that he ruins lives, not just careers. He says there might be danger for anyone involved with him."

Chloe snorts, rolling her eyes. "My father's a jerk. We all know that."

"But it's more than that," I continue, watching her carefully. "He's convinced that your father will...will hurt me if I stay here. He believes it's already too late for your mother." I pause. "He was warning me to leave."

Chloe's face becomes guarded, withdrawn. "My father wouldn't hurt you—he's not a violent man."

"I know he's your father, and I know it's difficult to accept—"

"I'm telling you, that's not who he is. And I would know."

There's a note of defiance in her voice. How do I convince her that the man who raised her is far more dangerous, far more self-serving than she wants to believe? Is such a thing possible?

Just then, there's a knock on Chloe's bedroom door.

"Emily, are you in there?"

It's Lena. I glance at Chloe, whose eyes are wide. "Just a minute!" I call as I hurry out of the bathroom, trying not to make any noise. Chloe darts toward the bed, flinging herself beneath the covers.

"Just a minute, Lena," I repeat, giving Chloe a silent nod before opening the door.

Lena's stern face softens for a moment, her gaze sweeping over me in an unspoken assessment. "Alicia needs you," she says abruptly, her gaze flicking over Chloe's prone form in the bed. "She's asking for you."

"Did she say why?"

Lena stares me down, as if to say I have no right to ask for an explanation.

"I'll head to her room immediately," I say.

Lena gives me another long, inscrutable look before stepping back to let me pass. As I walk down the hallway, I can't help but feel an increased sense of unease. What could Alicia possibly want with me? She's never asked for me before.

As I enter her room, I find her sitting in a high-backed chair by the window, her back towards me. The heavy curtains are drawn apart just enough to let a thin ray of sunlight in, illuminating the gloomy room with a soft ethereal glow.

"Alicia," I call softly, making sure not to startle her.

She doesn't turn around, doesn't acknowledge me at all. As I edge closer, inspecting her from behind, it's almost as if I'm looking at a statue rather than a living being.

"Alicia?" I repeat, my voice shaking slightly. The situation is eerie—even more so given the warnings of Marcus and Trevor echoing in my mind.

Suddenly, I can almost see the invisible chains that bind her to this room, this house. Chains made of fear, guilt and loss. Chains forged by Nathan Sterling.

"Alicia," I urge again, slowly reaching out to touch her shoulder. She flinches at my touch, but doesn't turn. "What's wrong?"

She doesn't answer right away. She just sits there in silence, her posture rigid, eyes fixed on the outside world she has forsaken. And then finally she blinks and turns toward me, her eyebrows rising in an expression of pleasant expectation.

"Sorry, dear," she says. "I didn't hear you come in. How are you?"

"I'm fine," I say, puzzled. "Is everything alright?"

"Of course. Why?" She blinks at me, a picture of innocence. Before I can think of anything to say, there's a quick rap on the door and Dr. Raymond Harris enters.

"Morning, Alicia," he says, smiling as he strides toward us.

"Good morning, Dr. Harris," Alicia says. Her voice is quiet but there's a certain hardness to it that I instantly notice.

Dr. Harris glances at me, giving me a quick nod before turning his attention back to Alicia. "I hear we've been having nightmares."

Alicia gives a noncommittal shrug, as though it's of little consequence. "It was nothing, really."

Whom did Alicia tell? Lena? And then Lena told Nathan, and Nathan called Dr. Harris? Why didn't Alicia tell me about this earlier, before I left to meet with Trevor?

Dr. Harris clucks his tongue. "Nightmares can tell us a great deal about the state of the mind, not to mention any maladies afflicting it. That's why I wanted to reassure you in person that I've adjusted your medication—it should help with the nightmares." He smiles.

He pulls out a form and a pen, then sets the form on the nearby desk. "If I could just have your signature here…"

Alicia takes the form from him without a word, her movements stiff and mechanical. I watch as Dr. Harris digs into his medical bag and brings out a small amber bottle filled with pills.

"We'll start with half a dose," he says, pouring out a single pill onto Alicia's trembling palm. "And if you feel better, we can consider increasing it."

The room is silent as Alicia looks down at the pill in her hand. Her fingers close around it, but she doesn't make any move to swallow it.

Dr. Harris seems unperturbed by her hesitation. "Why don't you take that now, Alicia? It should kick in within an hour or two."

There is a look of helpless defeat on Alicia's face. It's clear that she's used to all this: used to being told what she can and can't do, treated more like a guinea pig than a human being with dignity and value. As she opens her mouth to swallow the pill, I can't hold back any more. I grab her arm to stop her.

"Wait a minute, Alicia." I turn my gaze on the surprised doctor. "What exactly is this?"

He smiles condescendingly. "Like I said, this will help—"

"I'm not asking what it will do. I'm asking the name of the medication."

His smile fades, replaced by a thin line of annoyance. "It is called Medelium, Miss Just."

"And it's meant to help with nightmares?"

"Yes," he says shortly, the patience in his voice beginning to fray.

Despite my own rising anxiety, I push further. "Are there any side effects?"

For a brief moment, Dr. Harris hesitates before plastering on another one of his smiles. "Just some slight dizziness and mild fatigue, which should pass after a few days. But it's unlikely she'll even feel these things."

I turn back to Alicia, who's been quietly listening to our exchange. "It's your decision, Alicia. You get to decide."

As she stares at the pill, I imagine her tossing it aside and telling Dr. Harris that she's changed her mind—that she won't be taking any of his pills, come to think of it. I imagine the fire in her eyes, the horror and defeat on Dr. Harris's face…

But none of this happens. Instead she meekly opens her mouth, tosses the pill back, and swallows before staring out the window again.

Dr. Harris glances at me, eyes twinkling with triumph. "I hope you're feeling better soon, Mrs. Sterling," he says. "I'll update Mr. Davis on the new schedule." With that, he leaves.

Mr. Davis? Why would he update Grant?

Filing the thought away for later, I pull out my phone and look up the side effects for Medelium. It is designed to relax the body and increase focus, but the side effects include drowsiness, a sense of heaviness, anxiety, and even paranoia.

It gets me wondering: What else has the doctor been giving Alicia—and how much might her medication be responsible for her condition?

CHAPTER FIFTEEN

My mind is buzzing with so many questions that I can hardly think straight.

As Alicia slips back under the covers of her bed (she doesn't seem to stay awake longer than a few hours), I replay my conversation with Trevor Hammond, wondering whether I should really believe my life is in danger or if he was just being paranoid. Then, my mind skips forward to Dr. Harris's appearance and the new medication he added to Alicia's regimen.

What is going on in this strange place?

I feel restless, but I don't dare leave Alicia's room. She is surrounded by vultures, and I feel it's my duty to stay close and keep them off her. I am so angry with myself that I didn't stop her from signing that form Dr. Harris brought.

Then again, given the resigned way she took the pill, what are the chances she would've listened to me? She's been conditioned, like a jungle animal confined in a zoo. It'll take more than a few words from me to break her out of her paralysis.

To keep myself busy, I set about exploring her bookshelf. I've already tidied everything, but I haven't allowed myself the time to study her books.

There's a mix of everything—classic literature, modern novels, cookbooks, self-help guides. But mostly there are medical books. A glossary of anti-anxiety medications. A manual on managing agoraphobia. A book on cognitive behavioral therapy techniques. I take down one about the effects of trauma and flip through it absentmindedly.

As I read, I become absorbed in the text. The theories and treatments discussed are fascinating, but they also fire up my anxiety all over again. What if Alicia's condition is far more severe than I've been led to understand? What if Dr. Harris is not merely treating her symptoms but actively encouraging her agoraphobia for reasons I can't yet understand? The thought is so horrifying that I have to put the book down, my hands shaking as I do so.

I glance back at Alicia, her face a picture of tranquility in sleep. Whatever cocktail of drugs they've got her on, it gives her this eerie calm that doesn't seem natural. Whatever Nathan's reasons for controlling his wife this way, I now have no doubt that Dr. Harris is in on the plot.

Along with pretty much everyone else, it seems.

As I return my attention to the bookshelf, I notice a small notebook wedged between two hardcovers. It seems out of place amidst the well-read classics. Holding my breath, I pull it out and flip it open.

The pages are filled with Alicia's distinctive, looped handwriting. It's a journal, I realize. Here—here I will have real insights into Alicia's inner world, like the journal entry I discovered on her tablet. This book may hold the key to understanding what's going on—and what I can do to help her.

I glance back at Alicia, her chest rising and falling beneath the duvet. She stirs slightly but remains asleep. Taking a deep breath, I open the journal at a random page.

May 3rd

Gray skies today. I have to work so hard to be eupeptic on a day like this. Isn't that an interesting word, eupeptic? I just learned it recently while completing a crossword puzzle. Nathan keeps me well-supplied with crossword puzzles—he's very thoughtful that way. Honestly, I don't know what I would do without him. My own mind works to betray me, but I know Nathan has my best interests at heart.

I just wish he wasn't quite so busy with work all the time. I know his career is very important to him (to both of us, really), but when I think of the fun we used to have together, sailing and surfing and scouring the coastline for the best fish tacos...

The entry goes on in the same bouncy, schoolgirl-like tone. It's enough to make me sick. Have I completely misread the situation? Or does Alicia simply have no idea that her husband is the cause of so much of what she's going through?

I glance at the date again. This entry was written three weeks ago—and since I've been told she's been a shut-in for months...

I scan through a number of other entries, but all of them seem to be about Nathan, talking about him in glowing terms and expressing Alicia's desire to have a happy marriage with him again when she's 'cured.' The tone is strikingly different from that of the digital entry I came across.

Is this a red herring? After all, anyone who comes in here—Lena, for instance—could read this journal. Is it Alicia's way of playing along, making it appear she's harboring no suspicions toward Nathan?

As my curiosity overwhelms my caution, I begin searching for her tablet. I find it tucked under a stack of medical reports on the bedside table. I pick it up and glance at Alicia. She's still asleep, her face softened by the dim light filtering through the closed curtains.

Keeping one eye on Alicia, I open the tablet and navigate to the list of password protected documents. Then I glance over at the physical journal again, desperate for some help. It's lying sideways on my lap, and I go back to the entry I was reading before, picking up where I left off.

Hopefully, though, the clouds will clear soon. I feel so much better on sunny days—

especially when the wind is blowing in off the ocean, and I can smell the salt and

that light, refreshing scent that always transports me back to childhood. The scent is

inimitable—I've tried finding candles, even the really expensive ones, but they're all so

artificial and laden with chemicals. I guess there's no substitute for the real thing.

No matter. The important thing is to be optimistic, to think of all the things I have to be

thankful for. I have my health, a safe home, a loving husband and daughter. I am

happy: It's a state of mind, not a state of circumstance.

Until tomorrow, I will make the best of today. After all, cloudy days only make the

sunny ones that much sweeter.

As I stare at the words, a pattern jumps out at me. The first letter of every line, put together: H-e-t-i-a-n-t-h-u-s.

Is that a word?

I enter it into the digital journal as a password.

No dice.

Hmm. It's so close to being a word…but wait. If I use the second word from the third line, 'light' rather than 'that,' the word becomes 'helianthus.' Feeling certain I've heard the word before, I look it up on my phone.

It's the scientific name for 'sunflower.' Surely that's not a coincidence.

Excited now, I try the word 'helianthus' in the journal. Another failure. That shouldn't be a surprise, though—these entries have individual passwords, and 'helianthus' is probably just one password of many. I comb through the physical journal, searching for more acrostics, and come across several more botanical words: 'sequoia,' 'encelia,' and my favorite, 'echinocarpa.'

That gives me a new idea. I cross-reference dates and discover that many of the digital documents were created on the same day as the physical journal entries. I find the corresponding digital entry for the physical entry I was reading earlier and enter 'helianthus.'

This time it works. My heart flutters like a trapped bird searching for an open window, and the first words I read do nothing to calm it.

What to make of this Emily Just? She seems nice enough—a bit timid, a bit lacking in self-awareness, perhaps—but kind all the same. Still, there's that uneasy realization that he *hired her. Did he do so in order to keep tabs on me—as if the cameras aren't enough? Why did he choose her, and what instructions did he give her?*

I would like to trust her, but—

Alicia stirs in her bed, and I nearly hurl the tablet across the room out of fright. Taking a deep breath, I place it back beneath the medical reports on the bedside table, stealing another glance at Alicia to make sure she hasn't woken up.

Still sleeping.

With a thundering heart, I make my way out of the room. I'll have to come back later, while she's in a deep sleep, because I need to know what she wrote in those entries.

Her life, and mine as well, might depend on it.

CHAPTER SIXTEEN

Staring at the ceiling, I listen for any sound in the house: running water, the thump of a footfall, anything at all.

But it's silent. Graveyard silent, you might say.

I am far past the point of worrying about Alicia's privacy. Her safety is far too important to me. I'm sure that Nathan would use the same logic to justify his control of her, but the difference is that I actually have her best interests at heart.

And tonight, I'm going to get to the bottom of what's really going on here.

Easing my bedroom door open, I peer into the hallway to make sure it's empty. I'm aware that it's impossible to get to Alicia's room without being caught on camera, but I can only hope that the cameras aren't monitored constantly. Nathan hasn't confronted me so far, and I'm sure his hidden microphones have picked up more than a few interesting details he could use as grounds to fire me.

Maybe he only uses them to keep tabs on Alicia. And if so, surely he's not sitting up in the middle of the night, watching the cameras in her room. The man has a business to run—he can't spend all his time pouring over surveillance footage from his own house.

Swallowing my fears, I tiptoe down the hallway towards Alicia's room. The house must have been designed with stealth in mind because even my soft footsteps make no sound against the plush carpet. I pause outside her door, my ear pressed against the cool wood, listening for any sound of movement from within. All I hear is the distant hum of the mansion's air conditioning system.

I push the door open, wincing as it creaks.

Inside, Alicia lies still on her bed, her chest gently rising and falling with each breath. I can't help but feel a twinge of guilt as I watch her sleep. It feels as though I'm betraying her trust, and yet I remind myself that this is for her own good.

I shuffle towards the bedside table and quietly begin digging through the pile of medical reports. The tablet, however, isn't where I left it.

Panic pools in my stomach. I look around, double-checking the room, hoping to spot the tablet nestled amongst Alicia's numerous possessions. I can't find it anywhere.

Did Nathan take it? Is it possible he saw how I accessed Alicia's journal entries, and now those unlocked journal entries are in his possession? The very idea that I may have betrayed Alicia's sole source of privacy is enough to make me sick.

I turn in a slow circle, scanning the room helplessly, unsure what to do. Then, as Alicia stirs, I notice the tablet resting beside her, partially tucked beneath her pillow. Evidently, she must have woken while I was gone and picked it up. The relief at seeing it undisturbed washes over me like a wave crashing onto the shore.

Taking care not to wake her, I gingerly reach for it, my heart pounding with trepidation. The room suddenly feels smaller, the walls closing in on me. My breath hitches within my throat. One wrong move and I might wake her up and blow my cover.

She appears to be in a deep sleep, however, and I manage to reach under her pillow and gently tug the tablet free without disturbing her. Not wishing to press my luck any further, I hurry out and make my way back to my bedroom.

Once safely in my room, I lock the door behind me and exhale a breath I didn't realize I was holding. My heart is still pounding in my chest as I place the tablet on my bed and sit down beside it. Hesitantly, I power up the device and navigate to Alicia's journal entries.

It suddenly occurs to me that I should have grabbed Alicia's physical journal, as well—that way I would have the passwords for these digital entries. But it's too late to go back now. I'll just have to rely on the passwords I can recall from memory.

I decide to start at the very first entry, which was written about a year ago. I enter all the passwords I can recall, but none of them works, so I move on to the next entry. It's a painstaking process, but I have time.

All night, if necessary.

As I move down the list, my eyes start to droop and my head begins to feel heavy. I shake away the drowsiness washing over me, reminding myself that every second here is precious.

Finally, after several more attempts, one of the passwords works. My heart leaps in my chest as the text of an entry written nine months ago appears.

It happened again last night. I caught them together, N and R, practically knee to knee. R looked embarrassed, but N...he was almost defiant, like he was daring me to do something about it. Later, when we were getting ready for bed, I told him I didn't like how close they were getting, but he said I was worrying about nothing. He explained it all away, accused me of not trusting my own husband.

He has a way of getting in my head. I feel so sure about what's going on, and then he just talks and talks and makes me out to be the crazy one. He's been doing this for years now—ever since we got married—and if I let this continue much longer, I'll soon be unable to even think for myself.

He hasn't laid a hand on me, and he's never hurt Chloe. But it's very clear I'm a prisoner in this marriage while he has the freedom to do whatever he wants...even if that involves another woman.

I find another entry written shortly after the previous one. It begins with a long, rambling account of a disjointed dream she had, something that involved her becoming a bee and buzzing out into the rose garden, only to discover a giant glass dome enclosing the garden, so I skim on down toward the end of the entry and pick up after the dream.

He reassures me I'm not without friends in this house—tells me there are others willing to 'stretch out their necks for me.' But I don't buy it. This is between the two of us. Well, the two of us and Chloe.

Chloe—she's the reason I've stayed as long as I have. The thought of what she'd have to go through... Then again, what about what she's already going through?

It still galls me that her birth was used as an excuse to cut me out of the company. I was on bedrest for weeks, and by the time I was healthy enough to work again, I discovered the company had moved on without me. They took over the projects I'd been working on, said in the press release that I'd decided to "focus all my energy" on "being the best mother I could possibly be."

Yes, I was focused on that. But to say I couldn't also keep working with the company I'd been instrumental in starting was—and is—bullshit.

Enough with the ancient history. The bottom line is I won't take this treatment any more. I need to find a way to get an attorney to back me. But I must be discreet—if that man finds out, I shudder to think what he might be willing to do to shut me up.

That's why Chloe and I can't be here when he learns about it. We need to be staying somewhere else, somewhere far enough away that—

There is a scuffing footfall in the hallway. I stiffen, lowering the tablet and turning my gaze to the door. My heart, which was already beating at a frantic pace as I read the journal, now gallops within my chest. I listen for another sound, for the door handle to turn. For any sign that I've been discovered in such a precarious position.

Seconds pass. The hallway remains silent.

Still, I need to know for sure. Slipping the tablet beneath my pillow, I tiptoe to the door.

What if I open it and Nathan is standing there? What might he do to me?

Swallowing hard, I reach for the doorknob, my hand shaking slightly. The metal feels cold to the touch, and I take a moment to steady myself before turning it ever so slightly. There are no sounds from the other side, just silence. My heart is pounding in my chest like a drum.

With a deep breath, I muster my courage and pull the door open a crack. Peering through it, my eyes scan the dimly lit hallway, searching for any sign of movement.

But there's nothing. Just the familiar portraits along the wall, gazing down at me. I close the door again, making sure to lock it this time.

Is it possible I misheard, imagined the footfall? Maybe.

But as I turn back toward the bed, Alicia's words from her journal echo in my head: *I shudder to think what he might be willing to do to shut me up.*

CHAPTER SEVENTEEN

The next morning, I lie in bed late—not just because I'm tired from the late outing (I had to sneak Alicia's tablet back into her room, despite sensing someone was keeping tabs on me), but also because I can't shut my brain off.

Did Nathan find out about Alicia's plans to leave him and start doping her with medication to control her—medication that may have caused her agoraphobia? Is it possible that she was perfectly healthy, but he found a way to create a condition that would keep her under his thumb?

She probably wouldn't have taken medication from him willingly, not at that point. But if he slipped it into her food or drink without her knowing... It's a terrifying thought. And if it's true, it means I'm working for a man who is not only adulterous and manipulative but willing to cross both legal and ethical lines when it serves his purpose.

Suddenly, Trevor's warnings don't sound so far-fetched.

A rough timeline forms in my head: Around nine months ago, Alicia decides to work with an attorney and make plans to divorce Nathan because of his emotional abuse and unfaithfulness, as well as for cutting her out of the company she helped start. A few months later (about six months ago), she begins developing symptoms of agoraphobia—seemingly out of nowhere—and is prescribed a daily regimen by Dr. Raymond Harris. Rather than improving, however, her condition only worsens until she is a mere shell of herself, hidden away in her room like a ghost in a haunted mansion.

But why would Nathan do this? If he has so little love for his wife, why not just divorce her and move on with his life? He could even marry Rebecca Chen, if she was foolish enough to agree to it.

What is he so afraid of losing?

Then it hits me. There's only one reason Nathan would hesitate to divorce Alicia: because if she reveals that AltoTech was largely founded on her ideas, she might wrest control of the company from him—or force him to buy her out at a huge sum. They built the empire together during their marriage, so it would be difficult to argue she's not entitled to a substantial portion of it.

But if he can push her aside, keep her doped up and lethargic, then there's no need for a division of assets. And if anything were to happen to her…

A chill courses through my body. What if Alicia were to overdose on her medication? Given her wasted state, how difficult would it be to make her death look like a suicide? Then Nathan would be free of her for good, without having to sacrifice either his reputation or his empire. He would be pitied, the man who, despite all efforts, could not rescue his wife from the clutches of her own demons.

It's the perfect plan…or am I just being paranoid, connecting dots that aren't there?

Sitting up in bed, I massage my temples, feeling a headache beginning to form. My skin is clammy, and I'm certain I look as terrible as I feel. The thought of facing Nathan after last night is daunting, but I can't hide away forever—I have to get up eventually.

Besides, most days I don't run into him. Maybe he's already left the house.

Dragging myself out of bed, I head to the bathroom, splashing cold water on my face in an attempt to shake off the remnants of last night's fear. As I look in the mirror, the woman staring back at me appears frail, her eyes rimmed with shadows of sleepless nights and haunted by worry lines seemingly etched in by fear itself. I straighten up, forcing a mask of determination over my face.

I dress quickly and head downstairs, my heart pounding with each step I take. The house feels lifeless, haunted by more than just memories. The silence is only broken by the distant hum of kitchen appliances. I hesitate at the entrance to the kitchen, both longing for and dreading human contact.

Lena is busy preparing breakfast. She looks up as I enter, her face creasing into a smile that doesn't quite penetrate her eyes.

"Emily. I was beginning to think you'd come down with that sickness Chloe caught yesterday."

She's watching me closely, and I suspect she knows Chloe was only faking. But if she thinks I'm going to confess the truth to her, she's mistaken.

"Just lost track of time," I say, forcing a smile of my own. The lie feels heavy on my tongue, but I have no other choice. I can't let her, or anyone else in this house, know what's really going on.

"Sit," Lena commands gently, pointing to the breakfast table laden with toast and jam, crepes and freshly brewed coffee. The aroma is inviting, but my stomach churns at the sight of food.

Still, it's important to keep up appearances.

As I take a seat, she pours a cup of coffee for me. I wrap my fingers around the warm mug, drawing comfort from its heat.

"I've already taken breakfast up to Alicia," she says, her gaze never leaving mine. "No need to worry about her breakfast—or her pills."

"I'm sorry," I say, puzzled. "I thought that was my responsibility."

"It was."

I wait for an explanation, but none comes. Lena busies herself with breakfast again, carving into a pomegranate. Did Dr. Harris tell her that I had tried to get Alicia to refuse her new medication? Has she decided she can't trust me to do my job any more?

Before I can say anything else, Grant strides into the room. I smile expectantly, but he gives me no more than a curt nod before grabbing a cup of coffee. He seems distracted, upset, like he's just received terrible news.

"Grant," I call out to him as he walks away. He turns toward me, looking anxious and unsettled, very much unlike his usual self. "Is everything alright?"

"Just a challenging morning, Emily," he replies with a faltering, unconvincing smile.

With that, he exits the room, leaving me staring after him in confusion. What could have put him in such a mood?

"He's still very upset," Lena says as she resumes carving the pomegranate.

"Upset? About what?"

"You didn't hear?" She turns toward me, knife in hand. "An old friend of his died last night. Such a tragedy. Mr. Sterling is on edge, too. The man was a…family friend."

"Who?" I lean forward, my breakfast forgotten.

Lena is now scraping seeds out of the pomegranate with her hands. "A man by the name of Trevor Hammond. Used to work for Mr. Sterling."

My heart drops like a stone. Trevor Hammond? Dead? I met with him just yesterday—and ironically enough, he was warning me that *my* life was in danger.

I recall how he sat with his back to me, insisting that we talk without using names and that we don't look at one another. Was he murdered because he spoke with me?

Lena approaches me, a bowl in hand. "Pomegranate?" she asks. Before I can answer, she scoops a number of seeds onto my plate. They look like bloody teeth.

“What…what happened to him?” I murmur.

"Oh, he had some accident—apparently he was leaning out his third-story window, cleaning the outside of the glass, when he fell. The bottle of wine on the counter might have had something to do with it, I'm told."

I stare at my plate, unable to believe this news. The one person I've met who really seems to be looking out for me is now dead.

I need to talk to Chloe, see what she makes of all this. Because if Trevor really was killed for talking with me…

Then I might just be next.

CHAPTER EIGHTEEN

I am transferring Alicia's laundry into the dryer—I managed to snatch up Alicia's laundry basket before Lena could take that chore from me, too—when I hear Chloe enter the house.

I lower the lid of the washing machine and start up the dryer just as Chloe heads into the kitchen. I take a quick, steadying breath before following her in.

"Hey, Chloe," I greet her, my tone deliberately light. She glances up and offers a half-hearted grin.

"Hey, Em," she says, pulling a bottle of orange juice from the fridge. "What's new?"

I shrug one shoulder. "Nothing particularly exciting." I stare at her as I say this, hoping my eyes will convey the irony of my words. We are alone in the kitchen, as far as I can tell...but then again, is anyone ever really alone in this place?

She takes a long swallow straight from the bottle, then sets it on the counter and sighs. "Long day?"

"The longest," I say with mock relief. "If I stay here any longer, I'm going to go stir crazy."

She takes another swallow, then caps the bottle and returns it to the fridge. "I know just what you need. Follow me."

Intrigued, I follow her out of the room and to the front door of the house. We step outside. It's about four o'clock, the California sun still high and golden, the day crisp and dry.

"So where exactly are we going?" I ask, stealing a glance over my shoulder.

"Don't worry about the Nun," Chloe says with a dismissive wave of her hand. "She's busy playing Scrabble with my mom right now."

I frown at her.

"Just kidding. Mom hates board games. She's supervising the hanging of new curtains, from what I saw. That'll keep her busy for a while—she won't let the help out of her sight so long as they're in the house."

I nod, hoping she knows what she's talking about. "Where are we going, then?" I ask.

"There's a seafood shack just down the road—the Shanty, it's called. I assume you wanted to talk somewhere private?" She raises an eyebrow, and I nod, grateful she got the message.

“It’s…it’s about that man I met with yesterday.”

“The guy my dad fired?”

I nod. "He…he died last night, Chloe."

Chloe halts abruptly, her sneakers grinding into the gravel driveway. Her wide eyes meet mine, a mirror of shock and disbelief. "Are you serious?"

I nod. "Lena said it was an 'accidental' fall out a window, but the timing…"

Chloe's lips move to say something, but she quickly clamps them shut, her brow furrowed in thought. She starts walking again, her steps a bit more determined than before.

I want to hear what Chloe has to say, but I’m too impatient to wait.

“I think he was murdered for talking to me,” I say.

"Why? Who would do that?"

I stare at her, not wanting to say it.

"My dad?" She raises her eyebrows as if she can't believe what I'm implying. "No way. He may be a bit intense, but murder? That's just…insane."

I bite my lip, not wanting to push too hard, and we fall into a silence that stretches all the way to the Shanty. It's a cute little place with brightly painted tables and a view of the ocean. There are only a handful of other customers, so it's relatively quiet. It feels nice to be outside the confines of the mansion, even if it's just for a little bit.

"I'm telling you, he wouldn't do that," she finally says, after we've placed our orders and are nursing glasses of fresh lemonade. "He's my dad, Emily. I may not always agree with him, but he's not a killer."

I look at her, trying to gauge how much she really believes in what she's saying. The afternoon sun highlights the stubborn set of her jaw, and I can't help but wonder how much of this is blind faith, the kind of unwavering loyalty family often inspires.

"But has he ever done anything...anything that scared you?" I ask. I watch her face closely, observing the flicker of hesitation in her eyes.

Chloe looks down at her drink, stirring the straw around in the lemonade.

“What is it?” I ask.

Several long moments pass in silence.

"It's not relevant," she says, but there's no conviction in her voice. I wait, sensing that her own conscience won't allow her to keep quiet for long.

"My parents had an argument this one time," she begins slowly. "I came home early from school—this was, I don't know, seven or eight months ago—and I found them in the living room, shouting at each other. I'd never seen them fight before, not like this."

She picks at a chip in the paint on the table, her eyes focused on her hands, lost in the memory.

"I was standing at the door and they didn't see me," she continues. "I saw Dad grab Mom's arm. She flinched, tried to pull away."

She pauses, looking up to meet my gaze. There's vulnerability there, blinking against unshed tears.

"But he didn't let go. He didn't hurt her or anything... It was just the way he held onto her, you know? Like...like he could hurt her if he wanted to."

My heart aches for Chloe, forced to doubt her own father because of my suspicions. Her words hang heavy between us, a damning testament against Nathan Sterling. Suddenly my appetite is gone, the smell of the sea nauseating.

"What were they arguing about?" I ask gently. "Do you remember?"

"My mom was saying something about how she couldn't trust him any more, how he'd been lying to her and she wasn't going to be humiliated that way. He was telling her..."

Chloe shakes her head, her mouth twitching with sadness or anger. Or maybe both. "He was saying it was all in her head, that she was sick and needed help."

"How did it end?"

"Grant appeared and they stopped, both of them, just like that—like two school kids who'd been caught fighting." She swallows hard. "My dad was so angry—that's what didn't make sense to me. If he was trying to help her...why was he yelling at her like that?"

The question hangs between us, unanswered. Underneath her brave exterior, I see the flicker of fear in Chloe's eyes.

"I don't know, Chloe," I admit, swallowing hard against a knot in my throat. "But we're going to find out."

"We?" she asks, raising an eyebrow at me.

"We. We're going to get to the bottom of this together—and we're going to save your mother."

It's a brave thing to say, the right thing to say, and yet I can't help sensing I'm in way over my head. Here we are, she in her teens and me in my early twenties, talking about saving her mother from a potential plot devised by her own father. But as I look past Chloe's stubborn defiance to the underlying fear in her eyes, I don't care how strange this may feel. This is real, and terrifyingly so.

Something flickers through Chloe's eyes then, something akin to relief, before she quickly masks it with another swig of her lemonade. "So," she murmurs, "what exactly do you think is going on? You think my dad had Trevor killed because he knew things my dad didn't want anyone to know?"

I nod. "He seemed to believe your dad was involved in some illegal business practices.."

Chloe gives me a skeptical look but says nothing.

"More importantly," I say, "I believe your father is medicating your mother to keep her under control. I believe the medication she's on may even have caused her condition."

Chloe studies me, frowning. "How does that even make sense?"

"I think your father was slipping the medication to her without her knowledge. Then, as her agoraphobia developed, he brought Dr. Harris into the picture—and the medicating became official."

Chloe is shaking her head like she can't believe all this. "But how would my father even do that? It's not like he cooks her food."

"I think Lena's in on it, too."

Chloe's lips press together into a thin, tight line. "Lena wouldn't do that to my mother."

"What makes you so sure?"

"I'm telling you, she wouldn't do it, okay?" Her tone is sharp, and it's not difficult to make sense of her anger. In the course of one conversation, I've cast doubt on two of the most significant people in Chloe's life. It makes sense she'd push back.

"I know that all of this is a lot for you to hear—" I begin, reaching for her hand, but she pulls away.

"Don't coddle me," she says. "I'm not a child."

"I'm sorry. That wasn't my intention."

"There's a reason I call Lena the Nun, and it's not just her sternness. She has a code, too, and taking advantage of my mother that way would definitely break her code."

I blink, taken aback by Chloe's certainty. "You have a lot of faith in your housekeeper."

"That's because she's not just a housekeeper. She's a part of this family."

I consider this. Is Chloe right, and I've just misinterpreted Lena's behavior all along? Or has Chloe's familiarity with Lena blinded her to what's really going on?

“What about Grant?” Chloe asks suddenly.

I frown, surprised. "What about him?"

"You seem to suspect everyone else. Who's to say he's not part of the plot, too?"

I feel an immediate resistance to the idea…but is it based on evidence or emotion?

“Grant’s been quite open with me,” I find myself saying, brushing a few stray crumbs off the table so I can avoid Chloe’s watchful gaze.

"Oh, my gosh," she says as her anger dissolves, replaced by amusement. "You like him."

I look up at her, startled, heat rushing to my cheeks. "What? No, I don't—" But even as I say it, I know it (and she knows it): I do like him. He's been growing on me.

Chloe bursts into laughter, clapping her hands together with a glee that feels grotesquely out of place in the context of our macabre conversation. "Oh, this is too good," she crows, her laughter tapering off into chuckles. "You have a crush on Grant Davis."

The knot in my throat tightens. I swallow hard, pushing back a wave of panic. After Dillon, I've pretty much stayed away from the dating scene, and the thought of getting involved with someone like the charming, enigmatic Grant Davis…

It’s enough to make a girl’s head spin.

“The point is,” I say, doing my best to maintain what little composure I have left, “is that there’s really no reason to suspect he’s involved.”

“Have you shared your suspicions with him, then?”

“Well, no.”

She arches an eyebrow at me. "Is that because you don't want to ruin a good thing, or because you don't trust him?"

I open my mouth to speak, but no words come out. The truth is, I'm unsure.

"It's okay," Chloe says, shrugging. "We've all gotta do what we've gotta do." She checks the time. "We should probably get you back before Lena runs out of curtains."

We both rise. I feel anxious, though, unready to return.

"I'm worried," I say. "Not just about me, but about you, too."

She frowns skeptically. "You really think my dad's gonna hurt me?"

"I don't know what to think. Maybe not. But..." I shrug helplessly. "I wasn't trying to suck you into all this."

She chuckles softly. "I'm glad you did—it makes life so much more interesting. Besides, I have a panic button if things ever go horribly wrong."

"A panic button?"

Reaching into her pocket, she pulls out her phone. Then she opens her purse and pulls out a second one. The first—the one I've already seen—has a pink case covered in what are supposed to be glittering diamonds. The second phone is black, unadorned.

"It's what they call a burner," she says, the curl of her lips suggesting she's proud of herself. "After that fight with my parents, I got it just in case..." She trails off, frowning. "Anyway, the other phones connected to the house—they can be monitored by the house, blocked from making calls. But this one..." She shakes her head. "Nobody even knows it exists."

I shake my head, unsure whether to be impressed or dismayed at her foresight. "That's brilliant, Chloe." I meet her gaze, my heart heavy. "I just hope you never have occasion to use it."

CHAPTER NINETEEN

As we slip back into the house and go our separate ways, it occurs to me that if Chloe is right about Lena, then Lena could be a valuable ally. God knows I need all the help I can get in this place.

As much as Lena's behavior makes me suspicious, the truth is I'm only making assumptions about her motives. I caught her spying on Alicia's session with Dr. Harris, yes, but what if she was doing so for the same reason I stole Alicia's tablet and read her journal? What if Lena is just as protective of Alicia as I am, in her own way?

If that's the case, then it would be a shame for us to work against one another when we're really on the same side.

I decide to play the risky, delicate game of alliance. But I must approach Lena carefully. If she is, in fact, working against us—against Alicia, that is—then revealing my suspicions could put me in a precarious position.

Still, it's a risk I have to take—I need to find a way to shift the odds however I can before I end up like Trevor. I make my way to the kitchen, where I often find her at this time of the day. She's there, as expected, preparing dinner with an efficiency that is a master class in itself.

"Lena?" I start hesitantly, my heart pounding in my chest.

"What is it?" she asks without looking or pausing her work.

"I...we need to talk." My voice is low, the words barely escaping my lips.

She pauses then, a wooden spoon in her hand, and turns to face me. Her eyes are steady, her expression unreadable. I take a deep breath and plunge forward.

"I want to help Alicia," I manage to say. "And I think...I think you do, too."

Her eyes narrow ever so slightly, but she says nothing, waiting for me to continue. So I do.

"I'm worried about the new medication Dr. Harris is prescribing," I say, watching closely for her reaction. "Actually, I'm worried about all the medication Alicia is on. I think it could be having…adverse effects."

She cocks her head at me. "Are you a doctor?"

Heat prickles along my neck. "No, but I think—"

"Then maybe you should leave it to the professionals." She gives me a hard stare. A few days ago, I would have ended the conversation there, but now I sense this is a test. She wants to see whether I can be easily scared off or if I have the courage to stand up for myself.

"I would," I say, "if I was convinced they had Alicia's best interests in mind."

There are voices in the hallway—Grant walking past the doorway, on the phone with some business associate—and Lena's eyes flick in that direction. Lena waits for Grant's voice to fade, then says, "What do you know about what's in Alicia's best interests? You just got here last week."

"And perhaps that fresh perspective is exactly what's needed," I counter, keeping my voice steady despite my nervousness at contradicting this stalwart woman. "I may not have known her as long as you have, but I see her. I see Alicia. She's more than just a patient, more than a condition to be managed."

Lena returns her attention to the simmering pot on the stove. Her movements are mechanical, almost robotic, as she stirs without speaking. I take a deep breath and decide to push my luck a bit further.

"And I think you see her, too," I say quietly, trying to connect with her on a more personal level. "I think that deep in your heart, you know she's not being treated right. You know she's—" I stop abruptly, aware that Nathan could be listening in on our conversation. I need to tread carefully.

Lena says nothing for several long moments. Then she points at a shelf. "Fetch me that turmeric, would you?"

Puzzled by this transition, I rise and search the shelf.

My fingers brush against the smooth glass jar labeled 'Turmeric.' As I pass it to her, she nods her thanks, uncapping the jar and shaking a dash into the bubbling stew.

"It's hot in here, isn't it?" she says, dabbing at her forehead with her apron, though she doesn't appear to be sweating. She turns on the fan above the stove, which creates a steady hum that fills the air around us.

"This isn't an easy house to work in," she murmurs, her voice lower than before. Her gaze remains fixed on the pot in front of her.

"I'm starting to realize that," I respond cautiously, feeling my way through the conversation.

Lena continues as if I hadn't spoken. "Everyone here has their own tales...their own secrets." She stirs the stew slowly, deliberately. "And if you know what's best for you, you'll choose your words very carefully from now on."

There's no mistaking the warning in her tone. That must be why she turned the fan on.

Lena's attempt at disguising our conversation only bolsters my hope that she can actually be trusted. I press on, desperate for a listening ear.

"Alicia was going to leave Nathan," I say quickly. "She was talking with an attorney, making plans."

Lena stops stirring the pot for a fraction of a second. Then she goes on as if nothing happened.

There's a warning voice in the back of my head, but I ignore it. I need to get this off my chest.

"I think Nathan's been drugging her to keep her compliant," I say, lowering my voice even further. "Controllable. I'm not just theorizing here, either—I saw Alicia's journal entries."

Please don't think I'm crazy. Please don't think I'm crazy.

"Nathan?" She laughs humorlessly and shakes her head. "That...*doctor* is someone Grant found. And he's the one who prescribes the pills for the poor woman. Not Nathan. Nathan just trusts they're going to work."

I ponder that. It seems odd that Grant, rather than Nathan, should have so much say in Alicia's care. What am I to make of this? Is Grant hiding more than I realize, or is this just another case of Nathan delegating responsibilities he doesn't want to take care of on his own?

Or both?

Neither of us speaks for a long time. The soup bubbles and spits under Lena's watchful eye. I can't tell what she's thinking—her face is as unreadable as always. The silence stretches on, becoming unbearable. My heart hammers in my chest.

"You're playing with fire," she murmurs. "You're better off getting out of here while you still can."

"That's what Trevor Hammond warned me to do...and now he's dead."

The housekeeper takes a long breath. I can tell the gears are turning in her head. Have I made a mistake trusting her?

"Who else have you told?" she asks.

"Just Chloe."

"Not Grant?" She doesn't look at me, but there's a buried implication in her tone. Perhaps she thinks I'm emotionally compromised when it comes to Grant, as Chloe seems to believe.

"No," I say.

Lena fixes me with a long look. "Good," she finally says, turning her attention back to the pot.

"Why? Why is that good?"

"Don't trust anyone here," Lena says, sidestepping my question. "Not even Chloe."

I feel immediately defensive. "Chloe just wants what's best for her mom."

Lena shakes her head slowly, her eyes focused intently on the stew. "You see her mother in her, and there is certainly some of Alicia in Chloe. But there's some of her father in her, too. Gifted, but foolish. Easily led astray."

She ladles some of the stew into a bowl and hands it to me. "Take this to Alicia. And remember what I've said."

With that, Lena retreats from me, back into her world of pots and pans and spices, leaving me to ponder her words.

CHAPTER TWENTY

My sleep is restless, full of fragmented memories and snatches of conversation from earlier in the day.

I dream I am in the car with Dillon, and we're driving through the rooms of the Sterlings' mansion. Dillon keeps staring at me and talking to me, and I tell him to watch the road but he just laughs like it's all a joke, like there's no real danger.

We go through one room and the next, up and down staircases, watched over by the portraits of the Sterlings...only now every picture is the same picture of Nathan—stern, glowering, intimidating. As we move from room to room, the mansion starts to feel more like a labyrinth, and I begin to sense the walls are closing in.

"I want to get out," I tell Dillon, interrupting him. "Please drive us outside."

"Outside?" He looks at me quizzically, and now he's no longer Dillon. He's Dr. Harris, and he's holding a bottle of pills in his hand.

Suddenly, the car transforms into a couch, and I'm lying there, staring up at the ceiling. Dr. Harris sits across from me with a notepad and pen. The mansion walls are replaced by white padded walls that give off an eerie glow.

"Why would you want to leave, Emily?" he asks, his voice calm and soothing. "Outside is dangerous. Inside, you're safe. Isn't that what you want? To be safe?"

He shakes the pill bottle, and its rattle echoes around the room like a snake's warning. I feel the walls pressing in closer.

"No," I say, but I can hardly speak.

"Swallow this," says Dr. Harris, pushing a pill the size of a cucumber into my hand. "It will make everything better."

I toss the pill aside and rise, backing away in terror. I look around for some escape, but there are no doors in here, no windows—only the white walls and a single mirror.

Inside the mirror, Alicia peers back at me. *Help me,* she mouths, tapping against the glass with her fingertips. The force of her tapping causes tiny cracks to spread across the glass, as if she's a fish in an aquarium.

Or am I the fish? Are we both trapped in the aquarium?

The cracks run outward from the mirror and along the white walls, like I'm hatching from an egg. I step back again, and this time my foot catches on something and I sprawl on the ground. I raise my head to see a body on the floor.

It's Sadie.

The sight of her jerks me awake, and I throw my arms out and flounder around for my phone. The screen comes to life, giving off a faint glow, and I rest my head back and try to slow my breathing.

What was all that about?

I sometimes like to write down my dreams…but right now, the idea just feels exhausting. Instead I rise and peel back the curtain, staring out over the rose garden. Dawn is just beginning to break, casting an eerie half-light over everything. It's beautiful, in a haunting way. The promise of a new day. Feels like my life right now: stuck between the familiarity of my past and the uncertainty of my future.

I glance at my phone again, wanting to discuss the dream with Rich but knowing it's far too early to call. I can't help feeling that the dream is deeply connected to the mansion and its occupants. Could it be my subconscious mind trying to tell me something about Alicia and the Sterlings? Or am I just further spiraling into paranoia and fear?

The more time I spend here, it seems, the more my perception of reality blurs. The Sterlings' home feels like a maze of secrets, with me trapped in the center.

I sit on my bed, pondering Lena's warning about trusting Chloe. Chloe, Lena, Grant—there's no way to tell who's telling the truth and who's lying. I'd like to think I could read a teenager like Chloe, but I've been wrong before. It was Dillon who taught me that lesson, taught me that the people you're closest to can betray you in the worst possible way.

I rub my eyes, feeling a headache coming on. My brain is a whirl of thoughts and fears, all revolving around this house, these people. This job was supposed to be about taking care of Alicia, but it feels like I'm the one spiraling out of control.

I can keep talking to the same people over and over again, but it won't change the situation. Alicia will still be trapped here, doped up on God-knows-what.

No, I need to speak to the one person I've been avoiding, the one person who has the power to change the situation—and all the reason in the world not to. I don't expect to be able to convince Nathan of the wrongness of his actions, but if I secretly record our conversation, maybe I can get him to say something incriminating.

Something I could take to the police.

I get dressed, then pause at the door. Nathan Sterling. Tech mogul. One of the wealthiest men in the country, and now my employer. It would be easier to turn the other way, to pretend I don't see the signs, but I know I can't do that.

I wouldn't be able to live with myself.

Somewhere along the way, this job stopped being a job and became something more—a calling, perhaps, if that's not too pious. I have to help Alicia, even if that means risking my career.

And perhaps my very life, too.

It's still very early, but I have no interest in trying to sleep—not with that nightmare waiting in the shadows of my mind. Instead I leave my room and wander the house, letting it show me rooms and hallways I haven't previously discovered, immersing myself in the eerie silence that comes from being the only one awake.

My feet find their way to the library. I tell myself I came here to pass time with a book, but I know that's not true. No, I came here because it's next to Nathan's office, his *forbidden* office, and I would give anything to know what's in there—particularly what might be on his computer.

Does he keep a journal like Alicia does?

A light is on in the office—I can see the glow beneath the edge of the door. Unable to resist my curiosity, I move closer, wondering if Nathan is inside. Does he get up this early? How does a tech mogul start his day?

"Well, aren't you light on your feet," a voice behind me says. I spin around, heart thumping, to see Nathan standing there, staring at me with a mildly amused expression on his face.

"Mr. Sterling," I stammer, trying to steady my heart rate. "I didn't realize anyone else was awake."

"Just you, me, and the ghosts." I can't tell whether he's making a joke or not.

"Trouble sleeping?" he asks.

I nod and swallow hard. "It happens sometimes. Recurring nightmares."

He nods, running a finger over the spine of a book jutting out from the bookshelf beside him. "The best cure for insomnia is a clear conscience—that's what my mother used to say. You're not hiding anything, are you, Emily?"

The bluntness of the question takes me off guard, and I can only stare at the floor, chewing my lip as I try to think of an answer. I'd intended to record my conversation with him, but I can't exactly pull out my phone and start recording now.

"Relax," he says, smiling. "It was only a joke. Besides, your poker face isn't worth shit. I don't think you could bluff to save your life—and that's a compliment. A little honesty goes a long way when you're surrounded by rogues."

He's lost me now. Rogues? What is he talking about?

"Anyway," he continues, sighing regretfully, "I heard there was a bit of an…incident when Dr. Harris was last here."

Here we go. I decide to play dumb. "Incident?"

"I believe you tried to convince Alicia not to take her medication."

I smile as if to suggest the suggestion is ridiculous. "All I did was remind her that she has a choice about what she puts into her body. It's her call…and she decided to take the medication. I don't see what the problem is."

His nostrils flare in frustration. "Dr. Harris knows what he's doing—he came highly recommended. Grant knows him well."

That puzzles me. "Wait a minute. *Grant* hired him?"

Nathan waves a hand, dismissing my question. "The point is, you're way out of line here. It's not your job to say what medication Alicia should or shouldn't be on."

"I understand, Mr. Sterling," I say, trying to keep my voice steady. "But it *is* my job to ensure Alicia's wellbeing, and that includes supporting her autonomy and decision-making."

He looks back at me, something unreadable in his expression. "When has that been called into question?"

His words baffle me. He is a far better liar than I realized.

"I know what you're doing," I find myself saying. "You're controlling her." The words leave my mouth before I can stop them, a rush of adrenaline making me bold. "You're manipulating Alicia through fear—fear of the outside, fear of what you will do to her if she tries to leave you. Acting as if you're her savior when in truth...you're her jailer."

For a moment there's only silence. Nathan stares at me, squinting as if he can't quite believe what he's hearing.

"Why are you making me the enemy?" he asks. "I'm not perfect, sure, but I do love my wife. I've done everything in my power to take care of her, so why are you trying to stir up all this trouble?"

I stare at him, equally incredulous.

"Are you just envious of our success?" he asks. "Because we have all this, and you have…what? A bedroom in Townsville, Ohio?"

The heat rises to my cheeks. "This isn't about me! This is about what you're doing to your wife! It's not just theories, either—I have proof, and I'll go to the police if things don't change."

Nathan shakes his head pityingly. "If you think you're going to prove anything to the police, you're more deluded than I thought."

"Then I'll find a reporter! 'Tech Mogul Drugs Wife to Keep Her under His Thumb'—quite a headline, don't you think?"

Nathan stares at me for a few seconds in silence. "What are you looking for? A windfall from a lawsuit, perhaps? How much does your silence cost?"

I am trembling with rage. "I don't care about your damn money."

“Not even for your precious master’s degree?”

I say nothing. I'm not sure I could form the words if I tried, I'm so upset.

"Alicia likes you," Nathan goes on, "and for that reason alone I'm resisting the urge to fire you on the spot. I know how it would upset her." He raises a finger. "But mark my words, Miss Just: If you ever step out of line again, if you ever attempt to interfere with Alicia's medication or her treatment, you're through. I'm not going to warn you again."

“I’m not afraid of you.”

He recoils as if slapped. "I never wanted you to be afraid of me. I want you to be on my side, on Alicia's side. But I guess it's too late for that."

With that, he storms off, heading in the direction of Alicia's room. I stand alone in the library, trying to steady my breathing as I process what just happened.

I have no doubt that he will do as he threatened…but I can't let that stop me. Still, I had hoped that the threat of going to the police might have provoked a reaction, but he gave me nothing—a threat, certainly, but nothing approaching a confession of manipulating and controlling Alicia.

I sigh heavily. Dealing with Nathan directly won't work—he's too slippery for that.

But there may be one person who can get around his defenses.

CHAPTER TWENTY ONE

With Nathan's words still fresh in my mind, I make my way to Alicia's room. It's still very early, and ordinarily I wouldn't want to interrupt her rest, but this is too important to worry about propriety.

Alicia and I need to have a frank face-to-face talk. And if Nathan wants to spy on us, then so be it.

I knock gently on Alicia's door, my heart thumping like a drum inside my chest. The door opens just a crack, and her pale eyes peek out at me.

"Emily?" she asks, her voice sleep-thick and confused. "What time is it?"

"I'm sorry to wake you, Alicia, but we need to talk."

She pulls the door open wider, revealing herself in a silk nightgown. Her hair is tousled from sleep, and there's a vulnerability about her that makes the knot in my stomach tighten. She steps aside to let me in, closing the door softly behind us. As we settle into the plush chairs facing each other, I take a deep breath and steel myself for what's to come.

"Are you okay, Emily?" she asks with genuine concern. "You look worried."

I pause, choosing my words carefully. "When I first came here, this was a job, a way to pay for my master's degree so I could continue studying psychology. But this isn't just a job to me anymore. Something is wrong here, Alicia, and I can't just stand by and watch it happen."

Her brows furrow like chalk lines on a confused blackboard. "What are you talking about?"

I hesitate for a moment, mapping the best way forward. "I don't think you're sick, Alicia, at least not in the way everyone else does. I think you're being manipulated, controlled. And I think the person doing it...is your husband."

She stares at me calmly, giving nothing away. I supposed I shouldn't be surprised. After all, she must have suspected Nathan long before now.

I purse my lips. "You remember how, the other day, I asked if you knew Trevor Hammond?"

Her eyelids flutter, but otherwise she remains as still as a statue.

"He's dead," I say. "I believe he was murdered for talking to me—and that means your life could be in danger, too."

Alicia is silent for a long time. Her eyes, wide and unblinking, fixate on me as if I am broadcasting some obscure, foreign news bulletin she can't quite comprehend. Then, finally, she speaks.

"Nathan is...he can be very protective," she murmurs, her voice low and hesitant. Her gaze wanders the room, settling on nothing in particular. "He loves me...in his own way."

I fight the impulse to shake her. Is she playing for the cameras?

"This goes beyond protectiveness," I say. "He's a murderer, Alicia. And I believe he's been medicating you to control you, too. He claims he's treating your agoraphobia, but what if he's causing it?"

"I... I don't know what to believe," Alicia whispers, her hand trembling as she pushes a stray lock of hair behind her ear. "I've been so confused...so lost."

"It's not your fault, Alicia." The words tumble out of me. "Nathan manipulated you. He used your trust against you..." My voice cracks, and I take a deep breath, attempting to blink back the moisture gathering in my eyes.

She stews on this for a couple of moments, her fingers anxiously drumming on the armrest of the chair. I watch her swallow hard, the fear in her eyes contradicting the smile she tries to force.

"And if you're right," she finally says, "what do you want me to do about it? Go to the police? Everyone thinks I'm mad, soft in the head."

"Then we get you out—go to a hotel, if we have to. The important thing is to get you off this medication, get you beyond Nathan's reach so that he can't—"

"I won't go outside." Her voice is tight, her body suddenly tense and rigid, paralyzed by fear.

"You're going to have to conquer that phobia," I say as gently as I can. "I'll be right there with you."

She shakes her head vehemently. "I can't do that. You don't know how it feels—the thought of open spaces. It's like being trapped in a world where the sky is falling, and there's nowhere to hide. Like you're drowning in open air. Every breath becomes a struggle, every heartbeat a war drum in your chest."

I watch her as she describes her fear, the light in her eyes dimming with each word. I can feel her terror seeping into me like sweat, and with a sinking heart I realize she's not ready. She may never be ready to leave this house.

"But if you stay," I tell her, "this will just continue. Do you want to be his prisoner the rest of your life?"

"He needs to hear it from me." Her voice is low, and I lean forward to hear better.

"I've never really stood up to him," she continues. "I've always given in, taken his word for things. Maybe it's time I confront him—for myself."

She sounds resolved, but her fingers still grip the chair as though it's her lifeline. I tentatively reach out and place my hand over hers. The touch seems to startle her, but she doesn't pull away.

"No matter what happens," I tell her softly, "you're not alone in this."

She nods, a single tear slipping down her cheek. "I know. And thank you." The gratitude in her voice makes a lump swell in my throat.

We sit there for several long moments before I voice the thing I dread.

"And what if it doesn't change anything? What if it only angers him, makes his behavior worse?"

"Then you'll just have to leave on your own," she says softly, gazing toward the window. "Because if I can't get through to him…I'm never getting out of here."

CHAPTER TWENTY TWO

While Alicia and Nathan meet with Dr. Harris, I head to the kitchen where I find Grant standing with his back to me, pouring himself a cup of coffee from the high-end espresso machine. He's dressed in a navy suit and crisp white shirt, more formal attire than what he usually wears.

I listened outside Alicia's door long enough to get the gist of the conversation—Alicia's pleas, Nathan's denials, Dr. Harris's passivity. Realizing that talking with Nathan wasn't going to get him to confess to how he's been manipulating Alicia, I came up with a Plan B.

For a few moments I just watch Grant, preparing myself for what I'm about to say. There's something about Grant that causes my stomach to flutter with a cocktail of excitement and fear. I never know what to expect when I'm around him.

"Grant," I say, clearing my throat.

He spins around so fast, the coffee sloshes over the side of his cup. "Emily! I didn't hear you come in." His lips curve into that familiar charming smile, but his eyes betray his surprise.

"I need to talk to you," I say, holding his gaze. The nervousness bubbles inside me like a volcanic eruption, yet I manage to keep the tremor out of my voice.

"Of course," he replies, setting down his cup and drying his hand on a nearby dish towel. "What's on your mind?"

I pause for a moment, gathering my thoughts. He and Nathan are friends, and from everything I've heard, Grant seems to genuinely admire the man. How am I supposed to ask him to risk not only his job but perhaps his friendship as well, all in an effort to get Nathan to do the right thing?

"Can we go…somewhere else?" I ask, my gaze shifting to the windows. "Maybe out in the rose garden?"

He checks his watch. "Well, I have a meeting in twenty minutes, but...this seems serious." He takes off his jacket and throws it over the chair next to him. "Okay, let's go."

We walk side by side through the glass doors that lead to the garden. The sky is a clear azure, and the richness of the roses is almost overwhelming. Their sweet fragrance fills the air, and I find myself taking deep breaths to calm my nerves.

"Amazing, isn't it?" Grant asks. "How even a place as beautiful and expensive as the Sterlings' can feel stuffy after a while?"

I nod, but my mind is elsewhere, feeling out the path of this conversation. I can't make any assumptions here. Even if Grant is drawn to me the way I'm drawn to him, that doesn't necessarily mean he'll go out on a limb for me.

I decide to go for that universal masculine weakness: the need to play the hero.

"I…I'm in trouble, Grant," I begin.

His gaze softens. "What's wrong?"

"I didn't mean to get involved—didn't mean to take sides—but suddenly I find myself caught up in the Sterlings' marriage. Alicia is looking to me to help her, and I can't just turn away."

Grant's handsome face contorts with confusion. "You're a home aide, not a marriage counselor. Whatever's wrong in their marriage—and between you and me, it seems there's plenty—it's not your job to fix it. I would think Alicia would realize that."

I swallow hard, keeping my gaze steady on his. "She's desperate, scared of her own husband. He…he's controlling her, keeping her on medication so she doesn't have the clarity of mind to go through with her plans."

"Plans? What plans?"

"To divorce him. That's what she was going to do…and then he started medicating her, probably spiking her drinks."

Grant stares out across the roses, contemplative. I'm desperate to know what he's thinking, but I resist the urge to ask.

"Those are some serious accusations," he finally says. "How certain are you?"

I think of the journal entries. "Very."

"Why not confront him directly?"

"I have. He won't admit what he's doing."

Another long silence. I can't tell which way Grant is leaning, so I decide to give him one more push.

"I think he killed Trevor Hammond."

Grant spins toward me, frowning. "What are you talking about?"

"I met with Trevor the day he died. He warned me about Nathan, told me my life was in danger and I needed to leave. And then...he was found dead."

"That can't be. Nathan wouldn't..." Grant trails off, his gaze lost in the sea of roses. His face is a mask, but I can see doubt creeping into his eyes. The doubt I need him to feel, to question his loyalties and make a choice.

"I get that it looks suspicious," he said. "But the man was an addict—maybe you didn't know that."

The allegation surprises me. Trevor didn't strike me as an addict when I met him, but then again, it wasn't like I spent much time with him.

Or even got a good look at him.

"Kept all kinds of unsavory company," Grant goes on. "Maybe he cheated his supplier and got himself killed—who knows?"

"I thought you two were friends."

That catches him off guard. "We were," he says slowly. "I liked the guy—you couldn't help but like the guy. But when he started turning up stoned at work, making rambling allegations about everything under the sun—I had no choice but to cut him loose."

It's admirable, his refusal to believe Nathan was involved in Trevor's death, but it just doesn't add up.

"Trevor said he discovered something irregular," I say. "And he got fired because of it."

"Irregular?"

I shrug. "Something about back doors in the software."

Grant purses his lips in a thoughtful frown.

"If we can prove Nathan had a motive to kill him," I say, "then maybe we can convince the police to take another look at Trevor's death. I know he's your friend and trust him, but I'm telling you, he's the reason Trevor's dead. I know it."

Grant gazes off into the distance again, saying nothing.

"Unless you think you can get him to confess to you," I add. "You could try talking to him, secretly record the conversation."

He turns sharply toward me. "You're not recording this now, are you?"

"No, of course not. Why would I do that?"

He purses his lips again. There's a strange look in his eye, as if he can't quite decide what to make of me. Does he think I've lost my mind—or I'm straight up lying? Can't he see what's going on?

Grant looks at the house, as if expecting to see someone watching us. "Have you shared these theories with anyone else?" he asks.

"Yes, actually. Alicia, Lena, Chloe."

Grant shakes his head, his nostrils flaring. “You shouldn’t have done that. You should’ve come straight to me.”

“I know. I was just afraid that, given how close you and Nathan are—”

“You said he knows? You confronted him?”

I nod, uneasy at his agitated tone.

“Then we have to act quickly,” Grant says, glancing around. He takes my elbow and starts escorting me toward the driveway.

“Where are we going?” I ask. His fingers are uncomfortably tight on my arm.

“I’m getting you out of here.”

I dig in my heels. “No, I’m not leaving Alicia.”

“If he really is as guilty as you say, do you really think he won’t do to you the same thing he did to Trevor? He’ll just use a bottle of wine and some sleeping pills instead of a window. Is that what you want?”

His words send a shudder through me. His about-face, his sudden willingness to accept Nathan's complicity in Trevor's death, catches me off guard. But he's right. Nathan is dangerous, and there's no telling when he might try to get rid of me.

Still, there's something that scares me more: leaving Alicia alone with Nathan and losing any chance of bringing him to justice.

"I can't just abandon her," I insist, trying to pull away from him. But his grip only tightens.

He sighs in frustration. "You're not listening. This isn't about playing the hero anymore—it's about your safety."

"But—"

"But nothing," Grant interrupts, his voice rising above my protests. "You're going now."

He pulls me around the corner, and then we’re standing beside his black Audi, which reflects back the fire of the setting sun.

He pulls open the passenger door, looking at me with an expression I can't read. "Get in the car, Emily. We don't have time to discuss this."

"But I can't just—"

"You can and you will," he interrupts, his voice firm. "You are not safe here."

I look back at the mansion, its grandeur now tainted by the secrets it holds. I think of Alicia, alone and vulnerable in her room somewhere in that labyrinthine house. Of Chloe, just a teenager, tangled in a web of lies and manipulation within her own family. Of Lena, silently witnessing it all while keeping her own counsel.

And of Nathan, the man who holds all the cards.

Grant taps his fingers impatiently on the roof of the car. "We have to go," he says in a harsh stage whisper. "If he comes back and sees us now…"

"What happens to Alicia if I go?" I ask.

"I'll protect her," he says immediately.

"How will you do that when she won't leave the house?"

"I'll find a way, even if I have to tie her up. Please, Emily. You need to trust me."

Still, I hesitate. When I first came here, this was just a job, a means to an end. After getting to know Alicia and realizing her situation, though, this became something more.

A mission. A calling.

I hate the thought of leaving Alicia…but what if Grant is right, and my life is in danger? Can Grant really keep Alicia safe? I know Alicia won't leave this place willingly, and as long as she's here, she's in danger.

So how will Grant make sure nothing happens to her?

Grant, shifting impatiently from one foot to the other, seems to read the hesitation in my eyes.

"I'll get the police involved," he assures me. "I have a good friend on the force—he'll make sure Alicia is protected. But we need you safe too, Emily. And right now, that means getting out of here."

For a long moment, I'm frozen, torn between fear for my own safety and my sense of duty to Alicia. Then I realize Grant is right—risking my life unnecessarily won't help anyone. I need to get out of here.

But there's one thing I have to do first.

"I need to tell her," I say as I move toward the house. "I can't just leave without giving her an explanation."

"There's no time!" Grant hisses, hurrying after me. Just as I begin to open the front door, he slams it shut.

"Grant, just let me—"

"No!" His eyes are blazing now. "Listen to me very carefully. You are going to turn around, get into that car, and let me handle all of this."

"I just want to say goodbye—"

"You're not thinking straight." He grabs my arm again, his fingers as rigid as steel. "This is for your own good, Emily. You've gotten so wrapped up in this, you can't even think straight. I'm stretching out my neck for you—don't make me regret it."

I stare at him, puzzled. Where have I heard that turn of phrase before? I recall the entry from Alicia's journal and how Nathan used the very same phrase with her to convince her that she wasn't without a friend in this house. Only…what if it wasn't Nathan? What if it was Grant?

The journal didn't say Nathan's name, did it?

The realization hits me like a thunderclap. I just assumed the journal entry was about Nathan…but maybe I was wrong.

"Come on," he says, tugging me toward his waiting car. "We have to go."

"Trevor Hammond," I say. "He claimed he discovered some rather unscrupulous practices going on at AltoTech. You wouldn't know anything about that, would you?"

Grant stares at me blankly. "Where are you going with this?"

I am trembling like a leaf, but I will myself to continue. "He came to you with what he found, didn't you? And you…"

I recall Grant's words to me at the beach about making his mark on the world. "You couldn't allow others to know what was going on because it would ruin the company—and thus your future."

His eyes have gone matte, and his hand drops from my arm to hang limply at his side.

"You framed him and fired him," I continue, unable to stop myself now, "and you thought that was the end of it. But then he reached out to me…and that was when you knew you had to deal with him—permanently."

For a long time, Grant neither says nor does anything. Then a smile grows on his face. It is an unpleasant smile, a nasty smile, like a bully who has just watched the teacher hurry out and knows he has his victim all to himself.

"I was wondering when you would open your eyes and see what was right in front of your face," he says.

CHAPTER TWENTY THREE

It is as if the scales have fallen off my eyes. For several moments all I can do is stare at Grant in startled surprise, my mind working feverishly to put together the implications of this realization.

"You're the one who started doping Alicia, not Nathan," I say. "You hired Dr. Harris, you made sure she got heavily medicated. You knew that, because the company was founded on her ideas, she could claim a majority ownership if she divorced Nathan—and muscle you out."

Grant only stares at me, his amusement growing. It seems like he should be distressed at my revelations, maybe even angry, but he's remarkably calm. Does he know something I don't?

I go on, the words coming out in a rush. "Taking me to the beach—that was just your way of keeping tabs on me, extracting information. You had to know how much of a danger I was."

Grant snorts. "I should have drowned you in the ocean right then. That was my opportunity."

"So why didn't you?"

"I guess I fell under your spell."

I shake my head, unable to believe his callousness. When I met with Trevor Hammond, he refused to use names, and so I assumed he was talking about Nathan the whole time. But he was really talking about Grant. If only I had understood then....

"I almost ended it the night you took Alicia's tablet," Grant says. "I considered breaking into your room, putting an end to things right then and there. But that would be so...messy. How would I explain your sudden disappearance?"

I am only listening with one ear; my mind is still wandering over half-forgotten details. It occurs to me that Chloe was right about Nathan. For all his flaws and his controlling behavior, he wouldn't murder Trevor Hammond. He's not the type of person to get his hands dirty—or risk his freedom and reputation on such a gambit.

Grant, on the other hand...

"So what was your plan?" I ask. "If I hadn't interfered—would you have killed Alicia, made it look like a suicide?"

Grant shrugs one shoulder. "Something like that," he says with a casualness that chills me to my core. "Perhaps an accidental overdose. A grieving, mentally unstable woman loses herself in her medication...it would have been tragic, sure, but quite believable."

His words ring in my ears, and I can hardly believe what I'm hearing. This man standing before me, polished and polite Grant Davis, is a monster.

How did I not see through him sooner?

I gaze past Grant at the long road behind him, the road leading down the driveway and back to civilization. Back to safety. "I'm calling the police," I say as I dig my phone out of my pocket. My heart is fluttering like a distressed bird, but I force my hand to stay steady as I pull up the emergency number.

"Oh, are you?" Grant asks, his lips quirking in amusement. He takes a step closer, and I flinch back involuntarily. "Go ahead and try."

Before I can press dial, he lunges forward and snatches the phone from my grip. It falls to the ground with a clatter. Then he's on me, grasping my wrist in a vice-like grip. Panic surges through me, hot and violent like an electrical current.

"I haven't waited all this time," he says as I try to wrestle free of his grasp, "just for some home aide to ruin everything." His grip tightens, his eyes flaring with a dangerous intensity.

I kick out at him, but he sidesteps my foot easily. His laugh is a sharp, cruel sound—the sound of a man who believes himself to be entirely in control.

Still holding my wrist, he begins to drag me back toward the car. There's no question now what he plans to do—he's going to make sure I can never talk about what I've seen and heard. I'm not sure how he'll do it—whether he'll make me disappear or stage my death to look like suicide or an accident—but I know I won't stand a chance unless I can break free. My heartbeat pounds in my ears, every instinct screaming at me to run. But as hard as I struggle against his grip, he's just too strong.

"I trusted you," I say, hating the helplessness in my own voice. "I thought you were my friend."

My frantic eyes scan the area for a possible escape route: a car, a pedestrian, anything. But the Sterling mansion is secluded at the end of a long private road, far away from prying eyes.

"Funny notion, trust," Grant muses as he jerks me forward. "Quite overrated, if you ask me."

We are almost in the car now. No matter how hard I dig in my heels, I can't stop him. He's simply too strong for me.

Sucking in a lungful of air, I scream as loud as I can. No sooner have I started, though, before Grant slaps me hard across the face, causing me to stumble back against the door of his Audi, stunned and seeing stars. My face throbs where he struck me, the shock of the blow momentarily silencing my cries.

"Shut up," Grant says. His fingers dig into my arm as he fumbles for his keys, his gaze darting anxiously toward the house.

You're stronger than this, Emily, I tell myself. You have to be.

But no matter what I tell myself, no matter how hard I try to will myself to be strong and to fight back, I feel myself caving before Grant's unrelenting determination.

He opens the door and shoves me into the back of the car. I feel tears sting at my eyes as he slams the door shut, sealing me inside this metallic prison. The smell of cold leather and expensive cologne fills my nostrils, and I feel strangely resigned, as if I knew it would end this way all along.

I watch as Grant walks around to the driver's seat. Even now, he is completely composed—no hint of remorse or fear. Nothing but cold, hardened determination.

I close my eyes, a desperate prayer forming in my mind. Don't let it end like this. I can't die like this.

Suddenly, my mind is flooded with images of Sadie. Of her laughter and the long nights we spent talking about everything and nothing at all.

Her face swims before my eyes, as vivid and alive as the last time I saw her. No, not the last time—I can't bear to think of her like that, twisted and broken in the wreckage of Dillon's car. I imagine her as she was at her best: vibrant, full of life, full of dreams. Dreams that were snuffed out far too soon.

I think about the promises we made to each other, those whispered confessions under the cover of darkness when it felt like we were the only people in the world. Promises of adventure and freedom, of escaping Townsville and building a life for ourselves far away from the pain and hardship we knew.

Then I think of Alicia and what will happen to her once Grant is done dealing with me. He won't stop, not now that he's come this far. Alicia, trapped in her self-imposed cocoon, a prisoner of her own fears and insecurities. Will she be next?

Grant shifts into gear. My body coils, ready to throw open the door. If I can just get inside the house before he reaches me…

As the car begins to pull away, I see my chance.

And I take it.

I swing the door open and throw myself out. I lose my footing, scraping my knee on the asphalt, but then I'm on my feet again, racing for the front door.

Behind me, the car screeches to a halt.

Grant's footsteps chase me, but I've got a good lead on him, and I'm confident I can get inside the house before he catches me. If I can lock him out, keep him away while I contact the police…

I grab the door handle and yank. Nothing happens. I try again, but the door won't budge.

Locked? I see a face on the other side—Lena, her brow furrowed with worry, shaking her head as if to tell me I'm not allowed in.

Doesn't she see what's going on?

A shadow falls over me, and I turn around to see Grant standing there once again. "Oh, Emily," he says, shaking his head as he pulls a knife from his pocket. "You make things so complicated."

As I press myself against the door, watching the tip of the knife glinting in the light of the setting sun, I hear tires crunching on gravel.

Nathan has returned.

CHAPTER TWENTY FOUR

The knife disappears as quickly as it appeared, and Grant turns around, striding forward to meet Nathan.

"Back so soon," Grant says, a smile in his voice. "Did you get a chance to clear your head?"

Nathan is climbing out of his car. His eyes are clouded, his posture rigid.

"I need to get some work done," he says with a dismissive wave of his hand. He tries to brush past Grant, but Grant gets in front of him.

Nathan pulls up, realizing something is going on. "What's wrong?" His eyes slide past Grant to me, huddled against the door of his house.

"We have…a bit of a problem," Grant says. He lowers his voice, and all I can hear is a low murmur as Grant speaks. I can only imagine the lies he's telling.

I rush forward, hoping that—now that I know Nathan isn't the complete monster I thought he was—Nathan will realize what's going on and understand how Grant has betrayed him.

"Whatever he's telling you," I cry, "it's a lie! He's the one who doped Alicia, the one who caused her agoraphobia in the first place! And he murdered Trevor Hammond because he was talking to me—made it look like an accident, but the truth is—"

"Woah, woah!" Nathan says, holding up his hands as if to defend himself against the onslaught of words. "Slow down."

I take a moment to breathe, reining myself in. Nathan's dark eyes lock onto mine, filled with confusion and concern. I see no hint of malice.

Grant is quick to defend himself. "She's not well, Nathan," he says with a hint of concern in his voice that incenses me further. "She's been acting erratic all day."

"Erratic?" I say, my voice rising. "I'm not the one waving around knives and covering up murders. If Nathan hadn't arrived when he did, I might not be alive."

Grant shakes his head with a bewildered expression. "You hear how she talks?" he says to Nathan.

“That’s enough,” Nathan says to Grant, though his tone is far gentler than I like. “Let her talk.” Both men study me, waiting.

The silence presses in around us, the weight heavy against my skin. Everything depends on my ability to convince Nathan of Grant's guilt.

“The day Trevor was killed,” I begin, “was the same day I met him. He reached out to me, told me my life was in danger. At first I thought he was saying you wanted to hurt me, but now I realize he was talking about Grant.”

Nathan looks baffled. “Why would Grant want to hurt Trevor? They were friends.”

“Because of something Trevor came across—back doors in the software.”

Both men watch me in silence for several moments. It occurs to me that Nathan is waiting for me to go into detail.

“I don’t know exactly what he found,” I say, faltering. “But it must have been damning if it got him killed. Ask Grant—I’m sure he knows all about it.”

Nathan’s eyes shift to Grant. Grant smiles pityingly. "She's not making any sense," he says. "She probably invented the whole conversation."

"I knew we cut the odd corner," Nathan says. "Sometimes you have to do that sort of thing in business. But *murder*?" He shakes his head in utter disbelief.

“Please,” I tell Nathan. “We need to get the police. Grant is dangerous—there’s no telling what he might do now that his crimes have been exposed. I know you and Alicia have had your differences, but if you have any love for her at all, please protect her now. She needs you.”

There’s another long silence. The sun continues to sink out of sight, and the shadows stretch long. Why is Nathan still hesitating? Doesn’t he understand what’s going on?

Then I see it: the disbelief slowly giving way to anger. It occurs to me that he really was unaware of what was happening right under his nose. His jaw hardens and his nostrils flare as he turns to Grant.

"You're the one who recommended Dr. Harris," he says. "Why? Why were you so insistent she be medicated?"

"Nathan, surely you can see—"

"No," Nathan interrupts sharply. "Apparently, I can't see as well as I thought." I watch him, waiting for him to take a swing at Grant or declare that he's going to make Grant answer for his actions…but instead he simply breaks away and hurries toward the house.

"Didn't you hear what I said?" I shout at him, incredulous. "What are you doing?"

"I'm protecting Alicia, like you said I should," he calls over his shoulder.

And with that, he disappears into the house, leaving me standing there in the growing dusk, betrayed and alone. The chill of the evening air sinks through my clothes and into my bones. I shiver, feeling more lost than ever.

Grant pulls me roughly towards his car, his grip tight and unyielding. "You simply don't get it," he says, a smirk in his voice. "You think anyone cares what happens to you? You think anyone would notice if you disappeared?"

Panic flutters inside me. "Alicia would notice," I say, floundering for something to say. "When she realizes what you've done to me, she'll go to the police herself. You're through, Grant, one way or another."

He laughs and shakes his head as he tugs me forward. "You've got spirit, I'll give you that. But do you really think anyone would believe Alicia, a woman who can't even leave her room without a panic attack? She has no evidence, no proof—only the wild theories fed to her by her equally-unstable home aide."

As infuriating as it is, I realize he's right—people will believe him, not her. She can't stand up to Grant on her own. But the two of us?

It just might work.

"For what it's worth," Grant is saying as we reach the car, "I really did like you for a little while, despite your neurosis. If you had just kept your nose out of things that weren't your business—"

As he opens the car door, I make my move. I knee him in the groin as hard as I can, then jerk away, slipping from his grasp. He cries out and doubles over, clutching himself and cursing. I sprint towards the mansion as fast as my legs will carry me, heart pounding in my chest like a hammer.

I hear Grant behind me, his cursing replaced with growls of pain and frustration. It doesn't matter—I need to get to Alicia. A glance over my shoulder shows Grant recovering quicker than I'd hoped, getting back on his feet and starting after me with a determined glare.

The mansion looms ahead—locked, more than likely. But that's alright. I know a way in.

Racing around the corner of the building, I hurry through the rose garden on my way to the ivy trellis leading up to Chloe's bathroom. I can only hope the window is unlocked.

As I reach the foot of the trellis, I chance a look back. Grant is close behind, his face twisted with rage and determination. Fear gives me a surge of adrenaline, and I practically throw myself onto the trellis, climbing as quickly as I can. My fingers scrape against the wood, and with every second I imagine the feel of Grant's fingers closing around my ankle, jerking me back down to the ground.

I reach the window and shove it upward. It moves easily. Tumbling inside, I land hard on the heels of my hands, then rise and turn back to close the window.

There is no sign of Grant anywhere. Where did he go? To find a door?

It doesn't matter. If I can just find Chloe's burner phone, I can call the police—they'll straighten this whole thing out. Even if Nathan backs up Nathan, I have Alicia, Chloe, and perhaps even Lena on my side. It's our only shot.

I step out of the bathroom and into Chloe's bedroom. There's no sign of Chloe.

I move quickly, rolling back the pillowcases, lifting the mattress, and rifling through the drawers of her vanity trying to find her burner, all while casting wary glances at the windows and door in case Grant or Nathan should appear.

Finally I notice her purse at the foot of the bed. Of course! The one time she showed me her burner, it was in her purse. In all the stress and fear, I forgot that little detail.

Hurrying over to the purse, I begin to paw through it, unearthing lipstick, gum wrappers, an old movie ticket, a tangle of headphones, a jumble of receipts and candy wrappers…

My heart pounds in my chest as I tip the contents onto the bed, sifting through it all with shaking hands. The purse is small, so there can't be many more places for a phone to hide. I finish emptying the purse and pat the insides, but still I can't find it.

The phone isn't here.

CHAPTER TWENTY FIVE

I open the door of Chloe's bedroom and peek out into the hallway, looking first left and then right.

The coast is clear.

I close the door behind me and hurry to the right. Where, I wonder, is Chloe? Her purse is here, so I doubt she left the property. Is she grabbing food? Watching TV? Maybe working on homework in a quiet room?

Sweat begins to bead on my forehead. The silence of the house is broken only by the slap of my footfalls…until I begin to hear a second rhythm overlapping mine.

I spin around and see a figure approaching from behind—Grant. His hands are in his pockets as if he's simply out for a stroll, but the smile on his face reveals the lie.

"Where are you going, Emily?" he asks. "We didn't finish our conversation."

I dash forward, rounding a corner and racing down a hallway I barely recognize. The house seems twisted, unfamiliar, a maze designed to trap its prey. Behind me, Grant's footfalls echo ominously, a metronome of impending danger.

"Do you really think you can outrun me?" Grant calls from behind, his voice oozing with confidence.

He's taunting me, trying to work me into a panic. And it works. I'm gasping for breath, my legs turning to jelly beneath me. Surely someone will see what's going on and help.

But where is everyone?

I cut through a doorway, tripping over my feet as I enter a lavish dining room. A long table stretches ahead. The pristine white tablecloth, untouched by any crumbs or stains, throws the room's emptiness into stark relief. It's like a still life painting, a moment frozen in time.

"There you are," Grant says, his voice echoing through the empty room as his footsteps approach swiftly.

"Leave me alone!" I cry, hurrying through a doorway. "Chloe, Lena! Somebody help!"

There is no answer but Grant's laughter behind me. "I'm afraid they're a bit...*indisposed* at the moment."

Not bothering to ask what he means, I force my wobbly legs up the grand staircase. Before I know where I'm going, I have found my way to Alicia's room. Thinking to lock myself inside with Alicia, I grab the handle...

Only to discover the door is already locked.

"Alicia!" I cry, pounding on the door. "Let me in!" I steal a glance over my shoulder, expecting Grant to appear at any moment.

Come on, come on!

I beat the door with my fist. "Please let me in, Alicia! He's going to kill me! Grant is going to—"

The door rattles on its own. Then it rattles again.

"I can't open it!" Alicia says, sounding panicked. "He...he must have locked it electronically!"

I curse under my breath. Of course—Nathan gave Grant broad access to his company, so why wouldn't he give him access to the security features in his own home, too?

"Is there a way to override it?" I ask.

"Yes," a voice behind me answers, and I spin around to see Grant walking toward me. Now there's a knife in his hand, as if I needed any further confirmation of his intentions.

"It's very technical, though," he continues. "I could show you how, but what would be the fun in that?"

"Why are you doing this?" I say as I back away.

"Because you're trying to ruin everything. Do you have any idea what I've given to AltoTech? The sacrifices I've made? Of course, you don't—you can't. You breeze in here, a mentally-troubled young woman with a checkered past and a nose for everyone else's business, and you think you can bring me down? I won't let that happen."

I hold my hands up defensively, my heart thrumming like a wild bird in my chest. "Grant, you don't have to do this," I plead.

"Actually, I do."

He continues to glide toward me. Alicia is yelling something from behind the door, but my heartbeat is too loud in my ears for me to make out her words.

"Killing me in cold blood?" I ask, stealing a glance over my shoulder as I back up. "You'll never get away with it."

"I got away with Trevor, didn't I?"

"It's one thing to push a man out a window and make it look like an accident—it's something else entirely to make a stabbing look like an accident."

"You've got a point," Grant says. "I guess I'll just have to decide who killed you. Alicia seems like a promising candidate—unstable, highly emotional. Maybe you upset her with your wild, fantastical theories, and she got so upset at how you were slandering her husband that she decided to shut you up—permanently."

I shake my head. "Alicia's not capable of that kind of violence."

"Nobody is—until they do it."

As ridiculous as the idea is, I must admit that Grant can probably make the story sound convincing. And what better way to kill two birds with one stone? I'm gone for good, and Alicia is shuttled off to a psychiatric prison, thus removing the two people who can do the most damage to Grant and his precious AltoTech.

"And what about Nathan?" I ask, desperately trying to think of a way out of this situation. "What will he think?"

"He'll think what I tell him to think. If I say Alicia did it, he'll believe me—and be grateful to me for shielding him from all this. After everything that's transpired, whom do you think he'll believe? A mentally distressed wife or his steadfast right-hand man?"

"I'm not going to stick around and find out," I say, turning and running down the hallway. After being here about a week, I've gotten a feel for the layout of the place. My mind is so frantic and panicked, however, that all sense of direction abandons me, and I take turns at random, hoping to stumble across Chloe.

If she has her phone on her, I can call for help. Maybe she can help me outsmart Grant and buy time until the police arrive.

As I trot past a grand piano, I glance behind me. Grant is gone.

Is he flanking me? Preparing to ambush me as I pass a doorway?

I hurry on and eventually find myself in the kitchen, which appears to be empty. "Chloe?" I call. "Chloe—"

"Here."

I spin toward the sound. There, seated at a table, sits Chloe. Her face is pale, her back erect. Her burner phone rests in the middle of the table…

And beside her sits Grant, smiling at me.

"Nice of you to join us," Grant says. "Why don't you sit down and we can have a civilized discussion."

"I think I'll stand," I say, my voice quivering. My gaze flits between Chloe and Grant. The teenager's face is pale, her eyes wide with terror.

Grant shrugs, seemingly unperturbed by my refusal. "Suit yourself."

"Are you okay, Chloe?" I ask cautiously. She nods, but there's panic written all over her face. She's just as trapped as I am.

I turn to Grant. "This is between you and me. She has nothing to do with this."

"She does now," he says. "I caught her calling the police. The police! Now, why would she do a thing like that?"

Chloe's face crumples with misery.

"I-I didn't know what else to do," she stammers, her eyes welling with unshed tears. "I saw him chasing you, and…"

"It's okay, Chloe," I say. I need to buy time. I need to think.

There is a creak in the hallway. I glance that way, but I don't see anyone.

"What do you want, Grant?" I ask.

"Oh, nothing much," he says casually, his eyes like a predator's—calculating and cold. "Just your silence."

"If you let us all go, I won't tell anyone about your threats. You and Nathan can have AltoTech and all its profits—just let the rest of us go."

Grant chuckles. "That's very kind of you to offer, but I'm going to need you to do a lot better."

"What does that mean?"

"I want you to confess."

I raise an eyebrow. "Confess?"

"I want to hear you say you made it all up: your story about meeting with Trevor Hammond, the things about me doping Alicia. It's all a lie, and you know it. If you put that on record, then I'll let you drive out of here, safe and sound. Provided you never come back, of course."

"And Alicia? What happens to her?"

Grant's smile narrows into a thin line, his predatory gaze never leaving mine. "She'll remain here, of course. She's Nathan's wife, after all."

"You can't just keep her locked up here, drugged and confused," I counter vehemently, my voice shaking.

"She'll get the best care money can buy," he says with a nonchalant shrug. "You have my word on that."

His word—as if that's worth anything.

"And Chloe?" I ask, glancing at the terrified teenager sitting next to him.

"She will continue to grow up in her secure, loving home with both her parents." Grant's words are sickeningly sweet, honey coated in poison. "Isn't that right, Chloe?"

Chloe says nothing. She doesn't look at him, and I see her hands tighten around the edge of the table. It's clear she knows she's a pawn in Grant's game. I can only hope she won't have to pay the price for my mistakes.

I take a moment to consider his offer. If I confess, if I lie and say it was all a fabrication...Alicia will stay trapped here, slowly losing herself to the drugs that Grant has been feeding her. Chloe will grow up in a home where love is nothing more than a façade for control.

And Grant...Grant will get away scot-free. Even if I choose to believe he'll actually let me live, it's not much of a bargain.

But what's the alternative?

I look at Chloe, her eyes welling with fear, and I know I can't leave her here.

"I have another idea," I say.

He arches an eyebrow in expectant silence.

"You leave," I say. "You confess everything and you leave. You'll lose your share in the company, sure, but that's a small price to pay for a clean conscience."

For several moments Grant can only stare at me, as if waiting for the punchline of a joke. And then he laughs. It's a hollow sound, echoing off the mansion's polished walls, and it makes my blood run cold.

"Emily, darling," he says, slowly standing from his chair. "You really don't understand how this works, do you? I had hoped to come to a civilized understanding, but since you insist on doing things the hard way…"

He shoves the table against me, causing me to stumble backward. Then he's bounding toward me with the knife. I try to stand, but I'm too slow and I know that any moment now the knife will plunge into me. I anticipate the fiery pain even as I will my body to move faster.

Then, just as Grant closes the distance, there's a shout. Nathan barrels into the room and slams into him.

CHAPTER TWENTY SIX

I watch in stunned silence as Nathan and Grant tumble to the ground, the latter's knife skidding across the polished marble floor. Nathan is surprisingly agile, his eyes fierce and determined as he wrestles with Grant, who seems momentarily taken aback by his boss's sudden intervention.

"No more," Nathan manages to say, trying to get Grant in a headlock. "I won’t let you hurt this family anymore."

My heart pounds in my chest as I scramble to my feet, my gaze darting between the chaotic struggle on the floor and Chloe, who is watching with wide-eyed terror from her seat. It's a surreal scene, like something out of a nightmare, and I find myself rooted to the spot, unable to tear my eyes away.

Suddenly, Nathan cries out as Grant manages to shove him off. Grant scrambles for the knife on the floor, but before he can get to it, I lunge and grab it. My hand closes around the cold handle just as he turns back toward me.

"Emily," he says, panting heavily. His face is a mask of rage and disbelief. "Give me the knife."

"No," I reply, my voice surprisingly steady. I hold the knife out in front of me defensively.

Out of the corner of my eye, I see Chloe pick up the burner phone from the table and start dialing a number—hopefully, the police. I can't tear my gaze away from Grant, though, who's now on his feet and edging closer to me. His eyes are on the knife in my hand, calculating.

"Give me the knife," he says again, his voice a low growl.

"You're done, Grant," I say, trying to keep my own voice level. "It's over."

He chuckles darkly. "We'll see about that."

Suddenly he lunges at me, faster than I would've thought possible. I barely have time to react, thrusting the knife out in front of me. There's a sickening thud as Grant collides with the blade. He gasps, a look of shock twisting his handsome features. He stumbles back, clutching his side, where a dark stain is flourishing against his crisp white shirt.

“What have you done?” he whispers, touching the blood with his fingertips and staring at it.

Lena rushes into the room then, pale and breathing heavily. "What in God's name…" she murmurs, unable to finish the question.

“Lena,” I say as steadily as I can, “get Chloe out of here. Take her somewhere safe.”

Lena doesn’t argue. She grabs Chloe by the arm and pulls her out of the room. Nathan follows, casting a worried glance back at me, and I get the distinct impression that he wants nothing to do with what is about to transpire. The door shuts behind them, leaving me alone with Grant.

His eyes lock on mine, filled with a twisted mixture of rage and incredulity. I grip the knife tighter, my palms slick with sweat. My heart is pounding so hard I can hear it in my ears. I've spent so long feeling afraid—of my past, of my future, of this man bleeding out in front of me.

But I'm not running anymore. I'm not hiding. I'm not cowering. I'm standing my ground.

A strange clarity washes over me, wiping away the lingering fear and doubt. I don't want to live in the shadow of what happened to me anymore. I don't want to let the ghosts of my past dictate my future. And I certainly won't let Grant, or anyone else, control or manipulate me any longer.

"The police will be here soon," I say. “It’s over.”

He shakes his head, smiling bitterly. “No, it’s not. Not by a long shot.”

He staggers toward me.

“I’ll do it again,” I say, raising the knife in a shaky hand. “I swear I will.”

He swipes a hand towel off the corner of the table, then stretches it between his hands. “You don’t have it in you,” he says. “You’re not a killer.”

I swallow hard. Am I capable of killing him? If that’s what I must do to protect myself and everyone else here…can I do it?

He lunges, and I thrust the knife forward. He was only baiting me, however, because as soon as the knife is extended, he wraps the towel around it, then grabs my wrist and wrenches it hard. I cry out, dropping the knife and stumbling back.

Grant picks up the bloody knife, his smile cruel and triumphant. With the knife in his hands now, he steps closer. I back away, my breath hitching in my chest. I glance over my shoulder at the doorway behind me. All I have to do is keep backing away, keep plenty of space between Grant and me until the police arrive and—

"Close door," Grant says aloud, and the door behind me swings shut on its own. "Now lock it," Grant adds. I hear a faint whirring sound.

Suddenly, I've been backed into a corner.

Grant advances on me, the bloody knife gleaming in his grip. I can see the madness dancing in his eyes as he closes the gap between us. My breaths come in shallow gasps, each one burning my chest with icy fear.

"Looks like there's nowhere to hide," he says. "But don't worry—I'll make this quick and painless. Well, not really painless, but we can't all get what we want, can we?"

"Unlock door!" I say loudly. Nothing happens. "Unlock door!"

Grant smiles. "Only works with certain voices, I'm afraid. Mine and Nathan's. And I'm afraid Nathan isn't coming to your rescue any time soon."

"Maybe not," a voice says. "But he doesn't have to."

Grant and I both turn in surprise to see Alicia standing in the doorway of the kitchen. She is dressed in a nightgown, as if she's just woken up. Her hair is a mess, her cheeks pale, but her eyes are wide, alert, and burning with a fierce determination.

"Unlock the door," she commands in a clear voice. There's a whirr and a click as the door heeds her command.

"Alicia," Grant says, looking confused. "You should be in your room. You don't understand what's happening here."

"Oh, I understand perfectly," Alicia says, moving closer. "I understand you've been drugging me all this time. I understand you've taken an active part in my husband's unscrupulous business practices, and you want to have the company all to yourself. I understand you were instrumental in forcing me out of the company. I understand you murdered Trevor Hammond and intend to do the same to Emily—and perhaps the rest of us, as well. In fact, why not just blow up the house? You could say there was a leaky gas line."

"Careful, Alicia. You're sounding paranoid." Grant chuckles, but his eyes flicker nervously towards the door.

"Oh, not paranoid, just informed," Alicia answers. "I believe there is a difference."

It is so strange to see this version of Alicia: confident, powerful, unafraid. She stands there defiantly, not the fragile shut-in I know her to be, but a woman ready to face her fears and take control of her destiny.

Just then, Nathan walks in. He looks pale, and as he once more takes in the sight of Grant and the bloody knife in his hand, a shudder passes through Nathan.

"I guess this is your idea of handling things, eh, Grant?" he says.

Grant laughs. "Since when have you ever cared about anything but the bottom line? No, you've been more than content to turn a blind eye to my actions as long as I kept the profits rolling in."

Nathan's face hardens. "Get a hold of yourself! What are you going to do, commit *murder*? In my home? Haven't you done enough damage already?"

"I warned you not to trust him," Alicia says to her husband. "Way back in the beginning…I told you."

Nathan stares helplessly at her, almost as if he doesn't recognize the woman standing in front of him. How differently everything might have gone if he had simply listened to her.

"And you," Grant says to Alicia, shaking his head. "You had it so good. Married to the owner of a company worth nine figures, living in this palatial home. And you want to throw it all away—for what? A sense of justice? Moral superiority?"

"I want to be able to look at myself in the mirror again," Alicia replies. "You forced me out of the company I created, you duped Nathan—fool that he is—letting him carry on his affair while you corrupted the company. And then, just when I've worked up the courage to tell the truth, you have me drugged and convince everyone I'm insane."

She shakes her head, staring at Grant with a mixture of disgust and pity. "You must be the most miserable creature that ever lived."

Grant's eyes darken at that. Before he can speak, however, there's a loud knock on the front door.

"This is the police! Open the door!"

Grant's gaze flits to the hallway leading to the front door, uncertainty flashing in his eyes. He's cornered now, and he knows it.

"This doesn't have to get any worse than it already is," I say, raising my hands placatingly. "Just put down the knife."

"I'm going to let them in," Nathan says and starts to move, but Grant's voice stops him.

"Stay where you are!" Grant shrieks, gesturing with the knife. Nathan freezes, clearly stunned by the sight of the unhinged man in front of him.

"It's over, Grant," I say.

He takes a deep breath and nods slowly, lowering the knife. "You're right," he says quietly. "I guess there's no salvaging this situation. I'm going to prison for a long time, one way or another." He smiles weakly. "But at least I can get a bit of satisfaction before then."

With that, he darts toward Alicia. I cry out a warning, but I know I'm too late. Alicia is unarmed. She may have found her courage, but courage alone won't stop a knife.

Just as Grant is about to reach Alicia, Nathan steps into his path. The two men collide, and for a moment they struggle back and forth, wrestling for the weapon. Then Nathan sags to the floor, the hilt of the knife jutting from between his ribs.

"No!" Alicia screams.

Then boots are pounding across the floorboards as a trio of police officers enter the room. Grant drops the knife, raising his hands as the weapon clatters to the floor.

"I surrender," he says.

As one of the police officers cuffs Grant, I turn my attention to Alicia, who is crouched over Nathan. He is pale, even paler than before, and a bloody stain is rapidly spreading across his shirt.

He takes a deep breath to speak. "At least…I did something good before the end."

Alicia squeezes his hand, tears spilling from her eyes. And I can only look on, shell-shocked by the swift, brutal turn of events.

EPILOGUE

The Pacific Ocean is even more beautiful at sunrise.

It is my last day here, and I sit with my heels in the sand and watch as the first rays of light kiss the undulating waves. The air is cool and salty, filled with the promise of a new day, but I can only think about how much has changed since I arrived.

After everything that happened at the Sterlings' mansion, I felt the need for distance. Time to heal and to process. Time away from the chaos.

The media circus that followed the events of that night was intense. The unraveling of Nathan Sterling's empire made headline news worldwide. Alicia, despite her condition, handled it all with a quiet grace that I greatly admired. She attended each court session, refusing to hide even when everything became too much.

Grant Davis, I am told, will soon be behind bars for murder, attempted murder, embezzlement, and fraud. New evidence has surfaced, linking him to the death of Trevor Hammond, including a witness who spotted Grant's vehicle leaving the scene that night. Forensics also lifted a latent print that matches Grant's, and since he claimed to have never visited Trevor, his case isn't looking good.

Nathan, against all odds, survived the stabbing. The doctors said that if the blade had struck just a few millimeters to the side, it would have pierced his heart. He's in the hospital, under heavy security due to the onslaught of media attention and public outrage. He's on the mend now, slowly but surely, though his recovery is further complicated by the legal ramifications of what happened. The prosecutors want him in court; the doctors want him in bed.

Alicia, for her part, has made clear she believes her husband was largely ignorant of Grant's activities. She has filed for a legal separation from Nathan, a way to protect herself from further manipulation and abuse while also allowing the possibility of eventual reconciliation. I must say I have mixed feelings about this. Despite Nathan's heroic attempt to redeem himself, I would feel much better if Alicia made a clean break from him.

But she's a strong woman, much stronger than ever before. She's off her meds, and with the help of a new doctor, she's slowly pushing back the walls of fear that have closed in on her. I don't think she will ever let anyone control her the way she was controlled before.

The empire that was AltoTech is no more. Alicia and Nathan came to an agreement to liquidate the company and divide the funds, which was probably for the best, all things considered. This gives them each a chance to start fresh.

Chloe has been sent to live with an aunt in Oregon. Last I heard, she was adjusting well to her new life. She hasn't entirely forgiven her father for the lies and secrets, but her relationship with her mother is better than it has ever been, even if they only communicate over video calls and texts. It's good to see something positive come out of all this.

As for me? I'm still here, still standing. Rich, my therapist, says that's a victory in itself. And I guess he's right. But there are days when standing feels too much like sinking—when the weight of my past feels like it will pull me under for good.

And on those days, I remind myself of Alicia, of her courage and resilience. If she can go through all that and still have hope for the future…what right do I have to complain?

I breathe in deep the salty sea air and stare at the rising sun. It's a new day, filled with endless possibilities. For once, I don't let my past cloud my vision. I just let myself soak in the quiet beauty of the moment, relishing in the tranquility and solitude granted by the sandy shore and roaring waves.

Soon enough, it'll be time to say goodbye to my tranquil refuge. My temporary retreat has granted me the time to ponder and, in a way, heal. But life is waiting on the other side of this peaceful interlude. There's still so much I need to unravel—about myself, about the world and my place in it. There are connections to be mended and fears to be faced. But there's time. And, for the first time in a long while, I find myself looking forward to whatever comes next.

My thoughts are interrupted by the sound of someone clearing their throat behind me. I turn around to see Lena standing a short distance away, her hands clenched tightly in front of her. She looks troubled, uncertain of herself, very much unlike the stern, unflappable housekeeper I have come to know and grudgingly respect.

"I didn't mean to startle you," she says, her voice not much louder than the lapping waves. I shake my head, assuring her she hasn't, even though I'm still trying to quell the rapid beating in my chest.

She stares off across the sea, quiet and contemplative. "I suppose you're leaving soon," she says.

I nod. "Alicia's on the mend—she doesn't need looking after anymore."

"And I owe you a great debt of thanks for that. Truly."

I say nothing. Gratitude has always made me uncomfortable.

"I never wanted you to be here," she said. "From the moment you arrived, I wanted to get you out. I've seen how Chloe's been affected by living in that house—her father's passivity, Grant's scheming. I didn't want you to suffer the same."

"Is that why you were so hard on me?"

She chuckles softly. "I should have been harder—but then again, scaring you away seems like a losing effort."

"I'll take that as a compliment."

We both fall silent, watching the waves.

"There was something else I wanted to mention," she says, stepping closer. "Given the sensational nature of recent…*events*, you've become something of a celebrity."

I snort. "A celebrity? That's a bit of a stretch."

"Whatever you call it, my point is that someone reached out to me to ask about you. Someone offering a job.

I blink, surprised by her words. "A job?"

She nods, a rare smile playing at the corners of her lips. "It's for a family up in Oregon. The wife's a former model recovering from plastic surgery. They just need someone to give her a hand with the recovery process. They've heard about the work you've done here with Alicia and are quite impressed by how well you kept your head. And, given their social standing, I suspect they'd pay quite well."

A job in Oregon. The chance to put even more distance between myself and all that has happened here. To maybe start anew in a place where nobody knows my past. Yet, the thought of leaving also brings an unexpected wave of nostalgia.

"I see," I say, my voice barely audible against the crashing waves.

"Think about it," she says. "No need to rush into anything.

My heart hammers in my chest as the implications sink in. To help someone else, to enter another life filled with secrets and challenges...I'm not sure if I'm ready. My gaze drifts back to the horizon, a calm sea under an undisturbed sky—very much unlike the stormy waves of emotions churning within me.

"Thanks, Lena," I say. "For everything."

She nods, doing her best to assume a mask of stoicism, and turns to leave. Then she stops herself. "Oh, and if you do go," she adds, "be careful, will you? Everyone has their secrets, Emily—everyone."

I nod, taking her advice to heart. "I'll be careful."

Lena nods again, satisfied, and walks up the beach. I rise, dusting my hands, and turn to follow Lena, chased by the surge and sigh of the sea.

The sea that has no memory.

NOW AVAILABLE!

A TRUSTED STRANGER
(An Emily Just Psychological Thriller—Book Two)

"Amazing. The action simply didn't stop."
—Reader review for *What's His*

Home aide Emily Just's latest job brings her to a lakeside haven, catering to a couple swathed in bandages and vanity.

But beneath the glamorous surface of this image-obsessed couple's life, **Emily discovers a treacherous web of infidelity** that could turn lethal.

Struggling with her own resentment towards wealth, **she must navigate her own lens of envy** that could dangerously skew her perception of right and wrong.

Will **Emily be able to uncover the ugly truth in time to save lives—including her own?**

A TRUSTED STRANGER (An Emily Just Psychological Thriller—Book 2) is the second novel in a new psychological suspense series by mystery and suspense author Ella Swift. The series begins with A TRUSTED WIFE (Book 1).

Future books in the series are also available!

"A riveting read."
—Reader review for *What's His*

"An easy read and I can't wait to read the next book."
—Reader review for *What's His*

"Excellent. You can't help but like Peyton."
—Reader review for *What's His*

“It will pull you in from the beginning and not let up until the last paragraph. The characters are pretty true to life. A twist at the end will get you.”
—Reader review for *What's His*

“Very good book. It will pull you in from the beginning and not let up until the last paragraph. The characters are pretty true to life and it feels like you are there with them. A twist at the end will get you.”
—Reader review for What's His

Ella Swift

Ella Swift is author of the VIVIAN FOX suspense thriller series, comprising five books (and counting); PEYTON RISK mystery series, comprising five books (and counting); of the new COOPER TRACE mystery series, comprising five books (and counting); and of the EMILY JUST psychological thriller series, comprising five books (and counting).

An avid reader and lifelong fan of the mystery and thriller genres, Ella loves to hear from you, so please feel free to visit ellaswiftauthor.com to learn more and stay in touch.

BOOKS BY ELLA SWIFT

PEYTON RISK MYSTERY SERIES
WHAT'S HIS (Book #1)
WHAT'S LEFT (Book #2)
WHAT'S WISHED (Book #3)
WHAT'S GONE (Book #4)
WHAT'S MINE (Book #5)

COOPER TRACE MYSTERY SERIES
SHATTERED MIND (Book #1)
SHATTERED LIFE (Book #2)
SHATTERED HOPE (Book #3)
SHATTERED DREAM (Book #4)
SHATTERED FATE (Book #5)

VIVIAN FOX MYSTERY SERIES
ALL HE TAKES (Book #1)
ALL HE HIDES (Book #2)
ALL HE COVETS (Book #3)
ALL HE NEEDS (Book #4)
ALL HE DESTROYS (Book #5)

EMILY JUST PSYCHOLOGICAL SUSPENSE SERIES
A TRUSTED WIFE (Book #1)
A TRUSTED STRANGER (Book #2)
A TRUSTED HUSBAND (Book #3)
A TRUSTED FRIEND (Book #4)
A TRUSTED NEIGHBOR (Book #5)

Printed in Great Britain
by Amazon

44572717R00088